ALL THE BURNING ROOFTOPS

a novel

J. R. Klein

Publisher: Del Gato
Cover Image: NDTeam
Library of Congress Control Number: 2023911807
ISBN: 978-1-7368101-9-4
ISBN: 979-8-2182336-6-2 (ebook)

Also by J. R. Klein

Frankie Jones

The Ostermann House

*To Find – The Search for Meaning in Life on the
Gringo Trail*

A Distant Past, An Uncertain Future

The Code

The Visitor

Quarter Rats

Times Like These

If I Could Do It All Again

For Jeanne

This is a work of fiction. Names, places, and incidents are drawn from the author's imagination or are used fictitiously. Any resemblance to persons, living or dead, events, or locales is coincidental.

"No one leaves home unless home is the
mouth of a shark."
— Warsan Shire

"The American dream belongs to all of us."
— Kamala Harris

1

Armando Ortiz looked at the sky. It was clear. If rain were to come it would not happen for hours. But it was only seven-thirty; the summer weather was unpredictable. He always watched the morning TV weather forecast but it was usually of little help. It did not matter. He would be at work fifteen minutes early. He had arrived at work at least fifteen minutes early every day of his life since he was twelve when he started working in the clay tile factories in Saltillo. This was the habit his mother and father instilled in him nearly thirty years ago and he had never betrayed this habit—not in Saltillo, not now in Houston.

Hector Garza rode with Armando as they drove east along Holcombe Boulevard. The streets were clogged with traffic at that time of the morning, everyone in a mad hurry to be at work by eight o'clock.

Armando hated the madness of the traffic. It reminded him of the roads in Mexico when the workers burst onto the streets driving to the tile factories or the shoe factories or to the small offices where they worked.

Armando watched every car around him as he drove down Holcombe. Not just because he had no desire to have his eight-year-old Ford dented or scraped but because if that happened he knew he would have to show his license to the police and then the questions would begin. He used to worry about that, especially at this time of the morning. Whenever he worried he thought about his wife, Rosa, and his fourteen-year-old son Carlos, and his ten-year-old daughter Maria and their small house in the Hispanic part of west Houston. The thought of his family gave him courage.

As he rode down Holcombe he watched for the police cars that sat like motionless cats lurking in the strip mall parking lots. He knew why they were there at such an early hour. Some of them watched the movement of traffic looking for rude drivers and speeders, the ones who weaved quickly from lane to lane hoping to move ahead as fast as possible. Late for work, they hoped to make up time on the road. They might get stopped but rarely got ticketed—stopped long enough to guarantee that they would be late and make sure all their speeding and swerving was in vain.

But Armando also knew that some police were watching not just the movement of the cars but the people inside. They were the police who were adept at picking out immigrants and undocumented persons with remarkable accuracy—most of whom had recently arrived in the US. Those police could spot the uncertain looks on the faces of the drivers, the older cars, the ones with paper license plates—temporary tags while the permanent ones were being issued. The combination of that was the way the police could sort out who was who as people fled along the boulevard. Armando had a driver's license and always made sure it was in his wallet and that his wallet was in his pocket every time he left the house.

It bothered Armando the way some people were singled out but there was nothing he could do about it. He knew that of all the police parked in the strip mall lots it was often his fellow countrymen who were the worst, the most diligent at watching who passed down the boulevard early in the morning. This bothered Armando most of all because he knew they had the keenest eyes for the immigrants. It bothered him because he knew that many of those police were no different from the immigrants except that they were now citizens, born in the US perhaps. Or perhaps they became citizens after their parents crossed the border from Mexico and settled into the US.

Armando looked at the sky. The few clouds

remaining from the morning sunrise would soon be gone and the sun would begin to sear down on the city as it crept from the east.

Eyes set again to the traffic around him, Armando's mind drifted to what Rosa had said as he left the house. "Armando, on your way home be sure to pick up a cake for Carlos's birthday tonight." Thinking about that brought a smile to Armando's face. He would stop at Tres Hermanos Bakery and pick up a cake. Carlos was fourteen today and ready to start at Bellaire High School in a couple of months. Armando had never made it out of high school—the need to work in the tile factory in Saltillo made sure of that.

He laughed quietly to himself. Uneducated as he was, he could do any kind of labor with great skill. At times he had worked in construction in Houston. He could do carpentry, read blueprints, hang drywall, square a room, set hardwood floors, paint walls and trim, put in plumbing.

But now most days were spent putting shingles on rooftops. It was the hardest and one of the most dangerous jobs of all, especially when the temperature soared to a hundred in the shade and hit a hundred and thirty on the scalding rooftops.

The fragrance of laundry detergent lingered in Armando's clean t-shirt. Rosa made sure that he went to work every day with a clean shirt. It was a habit that all the Mexicans seemed to follow even though by ten or eleven in the morning their shirts clung to their backs, doused in perspiration. Yet Armando wanted to start each day with a clean shirt. It made him feel as though the heat on the rooftop might not overtake the whole day and that the heat was merely an illusion. He knew of course that the heat was real and that even a clean shirt would not make much difference.

Armando glanced at his watch. He passed quickly through the village of Bellaire heading into West University Place. He would arrive precisely as planned at seven forty-five. He would laugh and kid around for a moment with Stanley Jarkowski the owner of the roofing company. They might talk about soccer, the Houston Dynamo. And he would spend a few moments talking with the other workers before they climbed the ladder to the roof. All the workers were immigrants from Mexico and Central America, some having arrived very recently.

Stanley Jarkowski owned the Sunshine Roofing Company. Armando and Stanley got along well. Armando envied Stanley. Envied him not because he had a successful roofing company and never went a day without work but because of how easy it had been for him to move into American society.

Stanley was tall with pale blue European eyes and European features and a smooth jaw and a sunken smile and faint light skin. Armando knew that it had not been very long since Stanley Jarkowski's own family had arrived in America, that Stanley's and his father and mother were immigrants too. Armando noticed whenever a word slipped out that betrayed Stanley Jarkowski's roots or when one of the other construction contractors called him Stosh and then Stanley would laugh very hard and come back with a quick line in the native tongue of his parents. Armando could not understand what he was saying but he could tell that the words came as imperfectly from Stanley's lips as the Spanish that Armando's children uttered. Armando did not like that his children could not speak Spanish smoothly and effortlessly but he was glad that they spoke English without a trace of an accent of the kind that Armando had, the accent Armando would carry to his grave.

Armando did not like working on the roofs; he knew it was one of the most dangerous jobs of all. The inside work in the houses was the safest except at the very beginning when the framing was being done, standing on a two by four twenty feet over the ground while someone hoisted a beam up to you. Or straddling two beams while putting in a joist. That was worse than roofing—but not by much.

Armando had stayed with Stanley Jarkowski because he was usually fair to Armando and that alone made it worth it. The immigrants were frequently cheated by many of the other roofing companies. It had happened to Armando in the past especially from the contractors who drove along Westpark Drive on the edge of the city looking for day labor, picking from the men who gathered each morning waiting to be selected. Armando, too, had done that on many occasions when work ran thin or if it rained and he could not work on the roofs. He would wait with the others on the street corners hoping to be selected by someone who needed temporary workers. It was not easy for Armando to do this—to wait for a truck to come by looking for a few men. He felt like he was standing in a line-up in a police station as though he had done something wrong and yet all he wanted was work for the day.

Armando's sense of pride had been instilled in him by his mother back when he was a young teenager working in the tile factories. She would tell him, "Armando, do not be concerned that this is a simple ordinary job. It is a job that you must do with dignity. Because if you do not you will hate the job and then you will hate yourself for doing the work."

And when Armando's mother would tell him that, he knew that what he was doing was worthwhile even though the work was difficult and paid little and the factory was hot from the ovens that baked the clay tiles.

"When you have pride in yourself," she would tell him. "No one can take that away from you. If you let go of your pride it is hard to get it back because it once belonged to you and to no one else."

Armando Ortiz's mother lived that way her whole life, even while working six days a week as a domestic servant for a wealthy Saltillo family. She raised Armando and his brother and his sister by herself for many years after Armando's father died in a railroad accident.

Armando had lived in the US eighteen years now and he felt as though he belonged there. He had first gone to Corpus Christi, Texas, where he lived by himself in a small apartment. He worked at many different jobs and was happy to have work of any kind.

He missed his mother but was unable to visit her for fear of not getting back into the US. She was old and he knew she would not be around for long. He would remind himself that at least his brother and sister were there and that she was well taken care of. But that was not the same as being with her and seeing her smile and holding her hand.

He remembered how she would take the three of them to Mass at the Cathedral on Sunday. They each had special clothes that they wore only for the occasion. And afterwards on most Sundays she would make something delicious to eat—fried fish or tamales or a plate of enchiladas—and they would have a grand meal. And their uncle and his wife and their children would come over to share the delicious dinner with tortillas fresh and warm from the tortilleria down the street.

Or perhaps they would go to their uncle's house where they would eat a meal of pork posole. When Armando was sixteen he could have one of the good Mexican beers with his meal. These were his memories of that time and he knew they would stay with him forever no matter where he lived.

2

Shortly after Armando arrived in Corpus Christi he found a job working as a carpenter's assistant at a construction site. He was befriended by Luis, the job foreman. Luis liked how Armando performed every task with great dedication so one Saturday he invited Armando to a gathering at his place. It was there that Armando met Rosa, Luis' daughter. Armando thought she was the most beautiful person he had ever seen. More beautiful than any in all of Corpus Christi, more beautiful than any in Mexico. She had lush black hair and black twinkling eyes and soft brown skin and a smile that sparkled.

Rosa was lively and joyous and vivacious.

She said, "I like the name Armando very much. It is a wonderful name. I know that in Spanish it means man of strength…someone who is strong and brave. I like that. From everything my father has told me it is a perfect name for you."

Armando smiled but was too embarrassed to reply.

They spent the afternoon talking. Rosa had a way of making Armando laugh at the many wonderful stories she told. He secretly vowed that this was the woman of his dreams and that he would marry her someday.

Like the other workers, Armando usually brought his lunch to work. It was a simple lunch of tortillas with chicken boiled with cilantro and chopped onion and flavored with cumin and co-riander. He would shred the chicken and bring it in a container and make tacos at the construction site. Sometimes he would bring refritos—refried beans that he had made. He would spread the re-fritos on the tortillas with the chicken and add a piece of tomato and slice of avocado and more cilantro. He always brought fruit because it was cheap and healthy. An orange or a banana or an apple or sometimes a slice of pineapple that he bought at the market near where he lived.

Occasionally if he did not have time to pack lunch he would buy something from one of the food trucks that stopped each day at the construction site. The food was good and fresh and cheap. The tacos from the truck were a dollar twenty-five each. But his favorite of all were the tortas especially the torta al pastor—grilled pork on a toasted birote with a thin layer of refritos and a slice of avocado and onion and a dab of sour cream. A torta and two or three tacos kept him going for the rest of the afternoon. And he would drink a bottle of Fanta orange soda as he always had done when he worked in the tile factories.

Armando became friends with many of his coworkers and with the people who lived near him. He could tell a good joke and he liked to laugh. Nothing seemed to bother him. At the construction site there were large stacks of two-by-fours and four-by-fours and bricks wrapped in metal wire sitting on pallets. Armando would load lumber on his shoulders and carry it into the house or fill a wheelbarrow with bricks and roll it up a ramp into the house.

He did this all day and sometimes even hummed a song quietly as he worked. He remembered his mother saying, "Being sad and gloomy will solve nothing. You must face your problems with hope and a good attitude. It may not make your problems go away, Armando, but you will be able to put them out of your mind for a moment. And that will help."

Each day Armando kept thinking about Rosa. He wanted to ask her out but he was shy and afraid to ask until he learned that there would be a dance at St. Michael's Church in two weeks. He figured this was his best chance to ask her for a date, yet he knew he would first need permission from Luis, Rosa's father.

One day at work he mustered all his courage and told Luis about the dance.

"It will be at St. Michael's Church in two weeks, on the nineteenth," he told Luis. "I was wondering if it would be all right with you if I invited Rosa to the dance?"

Luis had confidence in Armando from the way he completed his tasks so thoroughly and always without complaint day after day. But Luis did not answer Armando right away. He decided he would wait a minute just to worry the young man a little before he agreed. Luis could not bring himself to wait longer. He looked kindly at Armando and said, "Weeell…it is Rosa you need to ask. She is the one who will let you know if she wants to go or not."

Armando grinned.

That night Armando called Rosa. His voice cracked as he asked if she would go to the dance with him. He cleared his throat and pretended not to be nervous.

"Well now, let me think about this. Hmm…I suppose going to a dance might be fun," Rosa replied slowly and coyly. "But I hope you are a good dancer because I am a *very* good dancer."

Armando was beginning to worry that she might turn him down.

Rosa laughed and it was a bright and cheerful laugh and Armando knew right away that she would go with him to the dance.

They talked on the phone for a half hour. As each minute passed Armando became happier to talk to her and he was more excited about going to the dance with her.

When he hung up, he immediately went to see what clothes he had to wear. He had told Rosa that the dance would be informal. Armando looked through his closet and dresser but found nothing suitable for an event as important to him as the dance. He had nothing to wear but work clothes and a pair of clean but faded jeans and a few faded shirts. *These will never do for such a big occasion*, he thought. He would buy new clothes. He wanted to be the best-dressed man at the dance; he wanted to make Rosa proud to be with him. Armando could hardly wait for the day of the dance to arrive.

At work Luis saw that Armando was in an especially good mood. He knew it was because Rosa had agreed to go to the dance with him. Armando joked with his fellow workers. They wondered how he could be so happy doing one of the most basic jobs of all.

Armando was paid on Friday. On Saturday he cashed his paycheck as soon as the bank opened and went straight to the store to buy clothes for the dance. He tried on several pairs of jeans and checked in the mirror to see which fit best.

Finding the right shirt was more difficult. He wanted a lively western-style shirt. The choice was not easy because there were many to choose from. Finally, he settled on a light blue one, cut trim in the waist but with ample room for his strong shoulders. It had dark blue and red embroidery across the two chest pockets.

He chose a leather belt with silver conchos and, of course, he bought a new pair of handsome boots. When he stood in front of a mirror in the store he liked what he saw. Most of all, though, he hoped Rosa would like it. This was an expensive purchase given his modest salary but he felt good about it nonetheless.

Armando called Rosa several times before the day of the dance. He feared that she might change her mind and tell him she could not go. But each time he called they talked longer than before and Rosa was more cheerful. Her voice rang with joy.

Rosa was eighteen. Armando was nineteen. She told him that she worked part-time at a restaurant and that she was taking courses at a local community college in the evening. She was not sure what she wanted to do with her life but she hoped to eventually get a college degree. Her father had told her many times that it was important for her to get a good education even though he himself had no chance to study beyond the eighth grade. Yet he had managed to rise up to his position of foreman as a construction worker.

Armando did not think he would be able to go to college. Like Luis, he had left school in Mexico at a young age. Armando frequently wondered if Luis would resent that he had little formal education, especially if he dated Rosa.

Yet, Luis seemed not to be worried about it. Armando realized that what mattered to Luis was how people do their work regardless of the simplicity of the task or the person's education. Armando liked that because it was the same simple and true message his mother reminded him of each day when he set off for the tile factory in the morning in Saltillo.

3

The day of the dance arrived. All afternoon, Armando's stomach fluttered when he thought about the evening ahead. He had a light dinner because he knew snacks and soft drinks would be available at the dance. He made sure he brought enough money to buy a treat.

At six o'clock he gave himself one last look in the mirror. He thought his new purchases were perfect. He hoped Rosa would approve. He was nervous but felt good. He would walk to her place barely twenty minutes from where he lived and then they would go to St. Michael's Church, a short distance from Rosa's house.

Armando stood for a moment on the porch

and then knocked gently but with confidence several times on the door. It did not take long for Rosa to open the door. There she stood—more beautiful than he could ever have imagined. She wore jeans, as new looking as Armando's. Like him, she had on an elegant pair of boots and a fine shirt with elaborate broidery. To top it off, she had a red bandana tied around her neck. Her dark black hair was held back with a shiny silver clip.

Armando could barely speak. The words seemed to stick in his throat.

"Well, maybe you came to the wrong house. I am expecting Armando Ortiz," Rosa said with meek laughter waiting for Armando to say something.

"Oh my, Rosa, you look wonderful!" he said.

Rosa called to her parents. "We are going now, Mama and Papa."

They walked down the street in the direction

of the church. The sun was setting. The sky had turned deep purple as the heat of the day wore off and the sun fell sheepishly behind the horizon. They passed houses in the neighborhood—a neighborhood where Rosa had spent her whole life. Her parents had rented the house they now lived in and when the owner put the house up for sale they immediately made an offer to buy it.

The area changed rapidly in a few short years. As more people from Mexico and Central America moved in more white people moved out. But it continued to be a good neighborhood with lawns and shrubs and bushes that were trimmed and houses that were painted and always in good condition.

The sun was gone by the time they arrived at St. Michael's. Already they could hear music coming from the gymnasium of the school where the dance would be held. There was a small line of people waiting to get in. Armando had picked up tickets for the dance as soon as Rosa agreed to go. The dance was free but the church wanted to make sure it would not be overcrowded.

The lights were turned down low inside the gymnasium where banners and streamers of all colors were strung across the ceiling. Armando expected that he and Rosa would be one of the first to arrive at the dance but the room was already half-filled and more people were filtering in.

The band consisted of three men and two women all dressed in traditional black and red mariachi costumes with sombreros and instruments—a guitar, a guitarron, a vihuela, a trumpet and violin. When they played they swung their heads from side to side and up and back to the beat of the music with shoulders that raised and lowered.

Armando and Rosa wasted no time getting on the dance floor. Rosa had been right; she was a very good dancer. Swinging and turning and floating with grace. The music became livelier as the band played many traditional folklorico songs and ballads and bursts of rousing mariachi songs.

They danced for nearly an hour and then Armando bought a soda for each of them and they watched the dancers. A couple, she with a beautiful flowing white full dress and he with classic Mexican clothes complete with a black sombrero, snapped to the music. She grabbed her dress and swung it gracefully before her. He danced standing tall with his hands behind his back as he tapped his black boots sharply on the floor with a rat-tat-tat to the beat of the music. Everyone clapped as they flowed across the dance floor.

"*Wow*, they are good," Rosa said. "I will never be so good."

"You are even better," Armando said quickly.

Rosa knew he was being nice but it made her feel special nonetheless.

Now, for the first time since coming to the US, Armando was more certain than ever that he had made the right decision to leave Mexico. Though he still missed his mother and his brother and his sister, Rosa's exuberance was infectious.

"You speak such good English," Armando told her. "I wish I could speak it like you."

"And your Spanish is so much better than mine. My parents are happy that my English is good but they wish I would do better with my Spanish."

"It is easy for you to fit in when your English is so good. I struggle and I am very conscious that I speak like a foreigner."

"I was born in the US. I am my parent's second child. Their first child, Leticia, was born in Mexico but she had a heart condition and medical treatment there was not good and unfortunately she died before she was one year old. When that happened my father decided to risk coming here with my mother. I was born two years after they arrived. I am a citizen but it took many years for my parents to become citizens. Now they are, and they are happy they came to America."

"You're very lucky you are a citizen."

"Yes. However, it is the only country I have known, I suppose you could say. Sometimes now and then we make a trip back to Mexico. I like to go there but I always know that my home is here in America, and that this is where it always will be."

"Someday I hope to be a citizen. And someday I would like to start a business," Armando said with conviction. "It has been my desire, my dream. All my life it has been my dream. Even when I was growing up in Mexico. I don't know what kind of business. Something in construction probably because it is what I know best and I am good working with my hands."

"My father said you are one of his best

workers."

Armando shrugged humbly and said, "I always try very hard when I am at work."

"Well, he doesn't say that about very many people. He expects all the workers to do a good job. So when he says you are a good worker he means you are better than the rest."

This made Armando feel particularly good because he knew Luis would never say it to his face.

"Oh, it's so nice to get out and do something special on the weekend," Rosa said. "The dance is perfect. My week is so busy. I have two courses at the community college. One is in American history and the other is in biology. I love both of them but my history professor is especially good. He is a great teacher and you can tell he likes to teach and that this is what he wants to do. It is easy to tell from the way he presents the information and the enthusiasm he has about what he is saying. Now we are learning about the people who came to America from Ireland and Europe in the nineteenth century. They were not treated well. It is very interesting to learn about that time."

"But now they are part of the country," Armando said. "And I guess that's why I came here. To be part of America. When I was growing up in Mexico, America seemed so far away. It was almost like something I read about in a story book, something unreal. And yet it was only a couple hundred miles from where I lived. But I decided to come. I crossed the border with other people. I didn't know who they were. I was frightened but once I got across I decided to come to the first big city I could get to. That's how I ended up in Corpus Christi."

"In history class we learned that many people came to America just as you did. Some crossed the border from Canada. Some got on boats that were going to Boston. Not everyone came through Ellis Island, that's where people were processed to stay in America. This is a big country and people came here however they could. From Russia and Poland and Italy and from many other countries. That's how it has been in this country for hundreds of years. That's what we learned in history class. I'm very glad you came to Corpus Christi. It's a good place to live." Rosa smiled a jovial smile and said, "And anyway, if you had gone to someplace else we would not be here at the dance tonight."

The night wore on. Armando and Rosa stayed until nearly the end of the dance. They walked out into the warm moist summer air. The smell of sea mist blew in from the bay. The sky was dark and dotted with a flutter of stars.

They walked down the boulevard. As they neared the corner where they would turn into Rosa's neighborhood a car filled with young men passed. From the window one of them yelled, "Get your brown asses back to where you came from, you spics!" He threw an empty beer can at Armando and Rosa.

Armando stopped and watched as the car sped off. Anger welled up inside him; he felt guilty thinking it was all his fault.

"Don't pay attention to them," Rosa said. "This is going to happen. I have lived here my whole life and it still happens to me sometimes. You never get used to it. You just learn to ignore it as best you can. When I was in high school some of the kids did this to us. And then a fight would start and everyone would get in trouble." Rosa became quiet. After a moment, she said, "I know how you feel but being angry will only ruin the great night we had."

They turned and walked down a street towards Rosa's house. Rosa could name almost every family who lived on the block.

She said, "My history professor told us how all throughout the past two hundred years hatred has been directed at one group of immigrants or another. He said people are always afraid that someone from another country will come here and take their jobs. But that doesn't happen because the immigrants always do the jobs no one else wants. He told us how when the immigrants came here from Germany and Russia and many other countries they went to work in the coal mines because very few Americans wanted to work there. And when the Irish came here after the potato crop failed they went to Boston. But the people in Boston wouldn't let them live there. They squeezed them into a few neighborhoods south of the city."

"I was warned about this," Armando confided. "I was even told that I was wasting my time coming here. But I don't want to take anyone's job from them. All I want is a better life. Not many people at the worksite want to do the job I do. But it doesn't bother me. I will do it as long as I have to," Armando said.

They stopped at a small park a block from Rosa's house and sat on a bench.

"Oh, it's so delightful here with the breeze and all, isn't it?" Rosa said.

Armando leaned back and looked at the black sky quilted with stars. "Yes, it is very beautiful," he replied softly.

"Sometimes at night I go out to the backyard and stare at the stars and think about my mother," Rosa said. "She died from cancer when I was twelve. From ovarian cancer and the doctors said there was nothing they could do because it had spread so much. It was a very sad time because I missed her so much."

"Oh, that must have been difficult," Armando uttered.

"Yes. When you are twelve years old you don't understand why these things happen. Especially to someone who is so dear to you. I remember walking down the street in front of our house and wondering how this could happen." Rosa stopped speaking for a minute and then said, "Well, my father eventually remarried. Her name is Gina and she is a sweet person. My father and her get along very well. Gina is always nice to me; she tries hard to be a good mother. I love her for that."

"I am glad for you," Armando said. "My father died when I was young. I don't remember him. My mother never got married again. She was always like a father and a mother both. She always knew how to find the good part of life. I don't know how she did it but she always did. I was never able to do it the way she could. I never had her…oh, I don't know…her wonderful outlook on life, her positive view of everything."

"Well, my father says you always have a good attitude. That's important to him because he is like that too. Perhaps he is a lot like how your mother was."

"Yes. In many ways I can see he is."

"Well, I would like to go to college and then maybe even become a nurse. When my mother became sick and died I made a vow to some-day…somehow, help people get through diffi-cult times like we went through. It was not easy for my mother at the very end."

An angelic silence settled around them. After a moment Rosa spoke, saying, "Wasn't the band great tonight, Armando? I love watching bands that play like that…don't you? They play so perfectly and it's so much fun to dance to the music."

When they arrived at Rosa's house they stood on the porch and talked for a long while. Both Rosa and Armando were happy to have gone to the dance. Armando hoped Rosa would go out with him again. In the dim porchlight he timidly asked if she would.

"Well, Armando Ortiz," she replied, "this was such fun, how can I say no? And you are such a good dancer."

He laughed.

Rosa smiled and said, "I work so hard during the week on my studies. On weekends I love to get out and have some fun."

That night, in the calm glow of the porch light, Armando was convinced that coming to America had been the right decision.

4

Armando could hardly wait for the day to end. It had been a very hot day. Nailing three-foot sheets of shingles onto the roof with an electric stapler again and again was exhausting.

On his way home he would stop and pick up a birthday cake at Tres Hermanos Bakery for Carlos's fourteenth birthday as Rosa had asked him to do before he left for work.

Driving down Holcombe he thought about his life during the past eighteen years: the year and a half he dated Rosa in Corpus Christi, their marriage at St. Michael's Church, their decision to come to Houston where they thought jobs for him would be better. And, of course, the happiness that always filled him when he realized that he was now an American citizen. His marriage to Rosa, herself a citizen, helped to make that possible.

He remembered the day he stood in the courthouse with many other immigrants, people from dozens of countries across the world as they proudly raised their hand and swore allegiance to the Constitution of the United States. It was a day that filled Armando with great pride and now he had a son and a daughter who were citizens also.

His job was difficult but he did it knowing that someday his children would not have to work like he did. They would go to college. They would get an education. They would work with their minds and not with their hands and backs. On those days on the rooftops when the temperature soared—each time he picked up a new shingle and nailed it to the roof one after another a hundred times a day—that was what he thought about, and it made the work bearable.

At the bakery Armando looked at the many cakes on display. There were so many delicious-looking cakes it was hard to decide but he was happy with the one he selected. He knew Carlos liked chocolate, so he picked one that had rich frosting. He had the words *Happy Birthday Carlos* added. He was sure Carlos would love it.

Armando walked in the door and set the cake on the counter and gave Rosa a kiss and then immediately took a shower to remove the sweat and dust that seemed to be permanently pasted onto his body by the day's heat. Oh how good it felt to put on clean clothes.

Every day at this time Carlos and Maria would come to the kitchen and talk with their father. Armando did not like to discuss his day on the rooftop. He preferred to imagine that he never did it. Instead he wanted to hear what Carlos and Maria had done that day. He would say,

"So what did you learn today?"

And Maria might say, "Well, I learned about geometry today, Papa."

Or Carlos might say, "I learned many things about biology…many things I did not know, Papa."

And usually Armando would say, "No, what I want to know is what did you learn about life? Today, what did you learn about life?"

Armando remembered how each day when he returned from the tile factory his mother would ask him the same thing. And though he was only placing clay tiles in an oven to bake she wanted to know what lessons about life he had learned from his simple repetitive job. She would tell him that life is very complex and that even when we do a simple task there is much to be learned from it.

And so Maria and Carlos and their father played this small game every evening. And then Maria might say, "Well, Papa, what I learned is that what I thought I knew I really did not know." And she would add, "You see, I studied very hard for my test today. And I did well on it."

A smile crept across Armando's face.

"But even though I got an A, I still missed a few questions. So what I learned today is that in life we might think we know everything. But we don't. It is impossible to know everything. Well…that's what I learned today."

And Rosa, who was listening as she prepared dinner said, "Yes, Maria, and it is important that we don't imagine we are smarter than everyone. Just because you might know many things there are always many things you do not know."

"Your mother is right," Armando said.

"Well, if nothing else I think I know what I want to do when I get older," Maria said.

"Oh, and what is that?" Armando asked with great curiosity.

"Well, I'm going to go to medical school

and be a doctor. Not just a doctor but a surgeon. We had a doctor come to school and tell us what she does. She is a surgeon. She told us all about her work and how satisfying it is to do something that helps make someone's life better. She seemed like many of the doctors Mama works with—the ones that Mama tells us about."

Rosa had earned a degree from the community college in Corpus Christi and then had gone to nursing school and now worked as a nurse at a hospital in Houston.

"Yes, many of the doctors at the hospital are very good and many are very caring. If you continue to study hard you too can be a doctor. But you will have to go to college and do well, and then you will need to go to medical school, of course. It will not be easy."

"I will study hard. I always study for many hours each night so I can be in the top of the class."

Nothing made Armando more proud than

knowing both of his children were good students.

"And you, Carlos my son, what will you be?"

Carlos was always less certain than Maria about his plans for the future. They seemed to change as frequently as the weather. But on this night he stated quite firmly, "I will become a US Senator."

"Oh, my word," Rosa blurted gently.

"Well, we have been studying all about the government and how it works," Carlos said. "Most students don't enjoy the class but for me it is one of my most favorite. What I know now is that if you are a good politician you can make a difference in the lives of people. A while back a member of the Houston City Council came to speak to us. It's not the same as being a member of Congress but he told us about all the issues and problems they deal with in a big city like Houston."

These were new versions of the many different ideas each of the children had about what they hoped to do someday. But it did not matter to Armando, he hoped that they would never sell out and do something less than what they wanted to do—less than what they were capable of.

"Now both of you, Carlos and Maria, please set the table and we will eat a delicious meal."

Rosa had made a large pot of *pollo con mole*, chicken simmered in rich dark *mole* sauce, a traditional meal for Sunday dinners and special occasions. It was Carlos's favorite dinner. The kitchen was filled with the wonderful scent of the classic Mexican sauce.

A large pot of the stew was set on the table along with a bowl of Spanish rice and a stack of fresh warm tortillas that Rosa bought at the tortilleria down the street. Armando said grace and the family dug into the wonderful meal.

Carlos had three helpings of his favorite dinner. Leaning back he declared, "Oh, that was delicious. I cannot eat another bite, Mama."

"Well, I hope you saved room for the best of all," Rosa said. She got up and brought the box of cake to the table.

"Okay, everyone," Armando said, "all together now."

Feliz cumpleaños a ti
Feliz cumpleaños a ti
Feliz cumpleaños cuerido Carlos
Feliz cumpleaños a ti

Everyone loved the cake. Carlos thanked his father for the delicious treat.

"Well, it's getting late. You need to go upstairs and get ready for tomorrow. Did you finish your homework?" Rosa asked.

"Before dinner," they both replied.

"Well, look it over again. It's best that you have everything just right and make sure you don't miss anything."

"We will," they told their mother.

Armando helped Rosa clear the table and wash the dishes. "Oh, my dear, it was a terribly hot day today," Armando told her.

"I wish you could find some other work to do. I worry all the time about the heat, or even worse, you falling from the roof," Rosa said.

"I've been thinking about maybe starting up my own company. After so many years of putting shingles on houses I know all the business angles. All it would take is a little money to get started."

"It will be a challenge. Don't you think?" Rosa said.

"Yes, a big one. But I've thought about it for a long time. In Houston new houses are being built all the time. The company Stanley Jarkowski owns is hardly ever without work. He always tells me about the other jobs he is working on and sometimes he even sends workers over to another house if he needs to finish it up. Of course, I would need ladders and shingles and a good truck…maybe even two."

"How will you get jobs?"

"I'll do like the other roofers do. Pass out flyers. Advertise in the local newspapers in Bellaire and West University, maybe in the papers south of the bayou. Stanley puts flyers on the doors of houses that look like they need new shingles. And I will get a web page on the internet. That will be important."

Now Armando was feeling very confident. "And to top it all off, I can look at a house and tell immediately what it needs. I know everything there is to know about putting shingles on a house. I know how to replace the plywood if you have to. Where to get tar paper and shingles including the ceramic and the asphalt ones."

This was not the first time Armando had told Rosa of this but she could tell now he was more serious than ever. Armando and Rosa always worked as a team with everything they did. They talked about it. Discussed the problems. Found solutions. All throughout their marriage they had done this when it came to the big decisions.

5

When Armando went to work the next day he found that Stanley Jarkowski had trimmed the work crew down from seven to five. No explanation was given. Armando had seen Stanley do this at other times. It seemed to be his way of getting the same output with fewer people to pay.

Although Stanley had only done this a few times in the past, Armando could not understand why he was doing it now. Armando made a silent vow that when he had his own roofing company he would never manipulate his employees this way.

The day was particularly difficult with less

workers. It meant fewer trips down the ladder for water and a shorter lunch time. Armando knew that the job had been moving along fine and that none of the workers were lazy. He knew that the two laid off workers would have to stand under the overpass by Westpark Drive or maybe wait at the end of the parking lot at Home Depot hoping to be picked up as day laborers.

At noon the workers came down from the roof and sat under a tree and ate the lunch meal they brought to work. Then they laid on the grass for a short but needed rest before climbing the ladder to the rooftop again.

No one talked of the missing workers. It was as if they never existed, as though they suddenly vanished from the planet. Everyone knew it was unlucky to talk about it because what they needed to do most of all was to concern themselves with their own precarious fate.

It was not until Friday, three days later, that Armando realized what Stanley was up to. When the crew was on its lunch break, Stanley pulled up in his pickup truck and paid them for the week's work. It was good to get a paycheck and fold it and place it safely in their wallets. As he handed out the checks he told them that he would be on vacation for the next two weeks. There would be no more work from him. It would be up to them to find work.

Now Armando knew why Stanley had laid off the two workers earlier in the week. It was clear that Sunshine Roofing would not be working the following week. Stanley did not want his workers leaving suddenly if they were aware there would be no work for them. His scheme fit together perfectly now. By laying off two men the others would have to work extra hard. The job would be finished exactly when Stanley had planned his vacation.

Armando felt betrayed as he drove down Holcombe that day on his way home. Even though Armando and Stanley got along well, Armando felt that Stanley did not have to lay off workers to guarantee that the job would finish by the end of the week. Everyone worked hard no matter what. Everyone knew what their specific tasks were. Even in the blistering heat the tiles were slapped down and stapled to the roof hundreds of times a day. No one complained.

It bothered Armando that Stanley never suggested other roofing companies that might need help, companies the workers might contact. Stanley could have done that. He was friends with the owners of other roofing companies. They occasionally swapped jobs if one of them could not get to it on time. But Armando knew that Stanley was afraid his workers might not return to him.

Despite Armando's sense of betrayal he remembered what his mother once told him. "Armando, when you think someone has treated you wrongly you must stop and try to figure out why.

And perhaps more importantly, think of what you might have done if the situation was reversed."

Armando made an effort to do this. If it had been *his* roofing company would *he* have done it differently? What if his company was very successful and was doing very well and what if Armando's family had moved into a bigger and more expensive house and Armando and Rosa had a big mortgage and Carlos and Maria were in very expensive schools, would he have done what Stanley did? *It is possible*, Armando told himself. Although he was an honest man he knew he was not perfect.

So now when Armando got home he would have to tell Rosa what happened, that he would not be working for Stanley next week. He never liked to give her news like that and yet he had to many times. It hurt his pride even though he knew he and Rosa were a team and that Rosa would still be able to work at the hospital. But the worst part was that he, like all the others, would need to find work for next week.

When he told Rosa about Stanley shutting down for two weeks, she said, "Oh, don't worry, Armando. We always get by. Always. And maybe this is a good time for you to take some time off. You have been working very hard and this has been one of the hottest summers ever. Every day I think of you on the roof with the heat and nothing to protect you from the blistering sun."

On Sunday Rosa got a phone call from Monica Sanchez, one of her fellow co-workers at the hospital. Rosa knew Monica very well. They had worked in the same unit for quite a while. Monica's husband worked in construction. Rosa and Monica talked briefly and then Rosa turned the phone over to Armando. Monica told him that her husband knew of a roofing company in need of workers on Monday. She gave Armando the address. Armando was delighted and he thanked her for the tip.

"There is a roofing job down in Missouri City," he told Rosa after he hung up. "I don't know, it might be a good idea to go. After all, work is work and a paycheck is a paycheck."

"Did she say which company it is? You know, Armando, you've had your share of bad companies to work for."

He assured Rosa everything would be fine, though in truth he had a gut feeling that he knew the company, Herrera Roofing. He may have even worked briefly for it at some time in the past. He hoped this was not true because of all the roofing companies in Houston it had a reputation as one of the worst to work for. He put the thought out of his mind and decided to show up in the morning regardless.

Rosa would have preferred for Armando to take some time off. She reminded him of that again.

Armando said, "It is either go to a job with

a chance of getting work or stand on the corner with the others. So…I'll go to the job. I'll be there at eight o'clock. Traffic on Highway 59 at that time of the morning is terrible so I will leave extra early."

Rosa nodded apathetically. "Bring water, do not forget that. It will be hot and not all the companies provide enough water. Fill up the large jug you have and be sure to bring it with you."

6

Armando was up at dawn Monday morning. Rosa packed a lunch for him and filled a plastic gallon jug with water and he was out the door with plenty of time to get to the worksite. The traffic on Highway 59 was bumper-to-bumper going seventy and seventy-five miles an hour. Armando hated these morning drives to a new job.

At Missouri City he pulled onto a main road that took him across town until he arrived at the house with the address. A new two-story house under construction. The kind Armando hated most because the plywood was easier to slip on than old shingles and he knew his balance, though good for his age, was not like when he was twenty-five. There were already several cars parked along the curb when he arrived. A small group of four men lingered in front of the house.

A gray truck with the words Herrera Roofing on the side and ladders strapped on top pulled to the curb. A man climbed out of the truck and strode pompously over to the men. Before a word was spoken, Armando recognized Manuel Herrera's portly round figure, the paunchy beltline, the ruddy brown complexion, the thin mustache. Armando knew immediately that this was the Herrera he had hoped he would not be working for that day. Everything was off to a bad start.

Herrera began croaking out orders in Spanish—briskly, rudely, sharply, occasionally stopping to spit onto the ground next to him. Now and then he would toss in a line in English. It was evident to Armando that Herrera's accent was just as thick as Armando's. And yet Herrera owned the roofing company. Herrera was the *heffe* whether Armando or anyone else liked it.

"All right, you bunch of stupid wetbacks," Herrera barked, cheeks puffed, lower lip gripped and tight. "You're going to get this job done and you're going to get it done on time and get it done right. Let's be clear. I don't give a shit if you think this work stinks, because I don't need you to do this work. Understand? People say you're taking jobs from whitey, from gringos. Ha, that's the biggest dumbest joke I ever heard." He let out a dark insulting laugh. "No gringo would ever do this shit work especially for what I pay," he said, and let out another dark insulting laugh. "You know that as well as I do and so I don't give a shit if you like me or not." He stopped talking and raised his small round shoulders. "No, I don't give a damn if you like this work or not. Why would I? There are a hundred slobs like you who would be happy to do it." He spit on the ground again, looked up to the roof, and said, "There it is. Now get the stuff from the truck and get your asses up there and get to work so I can make some money."

When the ladders and the shingles and the staple guns had been unloaded Herrera climbed into the truck. He stuck his head out the window. "I'll be back," he growled. "I've got another bunch of wetbacks to check on at my other job." He jammed his truck into gear and was off.

Armando checked the temperature on his cell phone. Eighty-six degrees at barely nine in the morning, and that was in the shade. On the roof in the sun with no shade, it would be in the mid-nineties and getting hotter by the minute. Now a part of Armando wished he had taken some time off as Rosa had suggested.

Two ladders were set to the roof. Three men climbed to the top. Staplers powered by electric cords on the ground were brought up. Stacks of shingles were carried up by two young workers. Bundles of shingles each weighing fifty or sixty pounds were held tight onto their shoulders as they climbed the ladder to the roof forty feet overhead, gripping the ladder with their other hand going quickly up rung by rung. One single slip, one single misstep, and they were on the ground with a broken leg or a broken arm or worse.

The bundle of shingles was passed off to workers on the roof and the men went down for another load. Over and over this was done. The shingle stacks were spaced apart on the roof for easy grab by the men with the staple guns. Slap a shingle on the roof. Snap, snap, snap three fast times. Another shingle, three staples. Another shingle, three staples. Snap, snap, snap. Another shingle. Snap, snap, snap.

Armando climbed the ladder and located a stack of shingles and picked up a staple gun.

The morning seemed to go on forever. At ten o'clock, one of the workers ordered everyone off the roof for a five-minute break and water.

It had been an unbearable day. Unbearable

because of the heat but much more unbearable because of something the workers learned about in the afternoon. Armando drove home in shock, barely able to pay attention to the flash of cars that sped past him. Barely able to think.

When he arrived home Rosa could tell he was not in good spirits. It had been an awful day and Herrera's attitude had made it worse, she assumed. Armando did not sit at the kitchen table and talk with her as he always did. He barely said a word before going into the living room. Rosa watched as he walked through the kitchen. She knew something very bad was bothering him. She went in and sat next to him on the sofa.

"There is something bothering you. I can tell. Let me know what it is. Maybe I can help."

Armando did not look at Rosa and this by itself told her that whatever was bothering him was very serious.

"Please, Armando, let me know what's bothering you."

Armando drew in a slow deep breath and let it out but still did not answer. After a long pause he finally eked out one word, saying, "Okay." Again, nothing. He set his forehead in his hands and stared at the floor beneath him.

"Armando, please."

"Well, there was a terrible, terrible tragedy today," he said and left it at that.

Rosa waited. "Where you work?"

Armando shook his head.

"Tell me. Please."

He looked at Rosa briefly then stared straight ahead and in little more than a whisper, said, "A man died today."

"Oh my God! How?"

"At one of the other companies a few blocks away."

Rosa felt life drain from her as she waited to hear the details.

"He was on the roof. A very steep roof two stories up and he slipped. Another worker reached to grab him but it was too late. He tumbled off the roof still carrying a sharp tile knife in his hand." Armando stopped speaking for a moment. "When he hit the ground the knife went into his chest. I guess it must have punctured his heart or something. That's all I know. They got him to the hospital very quickly…but…but it was too late."

Rosa's hands trembled.

"I can't say anymore. I need to sit here alone for a while," Armando said.

"I understand, dear. Please, don't go back there tomorrow. Please don't," Rosa said.

"It didn't happen where we were."

"I understand. But even so you don't need to work for a person like Herrera. He is a bad man and even if the tragedy did not happen at his company bad things happen around him. He treats his people like animals. No, that's not true, most people treat animals better."

"I must go back," Armando said softly. "Not

because of Herrera. But because of the other workers. They are short-staffed and everyone is working very, very hard. It is difficult to do the job with such a small crew. Herrera likes it that way because he makes more money. We all do some of everything…not like on other roofing jobs where we stick to one task. It is much better when you do that but we cannot do it on this job. What does Herrera care? He knows the job will get done no matter what."

"Why is it that some people when they come to America they treat their fellow countrymen so bad?" Rosa wondered.

"Because they think they are better…that's why. Herrera is an arrogant man. He probably has been an arrogant man his whole life."

"People like him make it difficult," Rosa said. "They make it difficult for everyone…and probably even for Herrera himself even though he doesn't know it. People do not want to work for someone like Herrera."

"But they don't have a choice. The paycheck is what matters. They all hate Herrera but they work for him when they have to."

"And they do a good job even when working for Herrera," Rosa said, "because they know that's what is expected of them."

"Yes, most of them do. And you're right, they have no choice. At noon when we sat under the tree eating our lunch everyone said this was the last time they would work for Herrera. But next week some of them will be back again because they won't be able to find other work. Herrera is not concerned if they don't come back because he knows he can pick up workers on the street corner. And they will come and do his work and get paid…maybe. And then it will start over again. It is a trap. But all I know is that tonight some place, at a home somewhere, there is a family with no husband, with no father. A family filled with grief in its heart because of what happened when the man fell from the roof and died. All that man wanted to do was make a living for his family. That I can be sure of or else he would not have been on the roof."

"You see, my love, it is time for you to find a new line of work. Remember when you worked in construction? On the indoor jobs where the work is not so hard? I tell you this all the time and you say you will but you don't."

"What I will do is start my own roofing company. Isn't that a good idea?"

Rosa sighed and said, "Yes. I've told you this before. But I still worry."

"You will always worry. Maybe it's good that at least one of us worries. It's important for one of us to worry a little. A little at least," Armando said with the first small smile of the evening.

"I suppose I have never had the confidence that you have," Rosa added. "It must have come from your work as a child in the tile factories in Saltillo."

"And from my mother. Don't forget her. She taught me to have confidence in myself no matter what challenges I face. When I would come home from the factory very tired and very disappointed with everything, she would say, 'Armando, if you believe in yourself, you will see the world through a new window. A window into which the sun always shines and the day is always bright.'"

"Your mother was a wonderful woman," Rosa said softly. "Oh, I wish I could have met her."

"But you are a lot like her," Armando said. "The way you help and encourage Carlos and Maria is just the same. So, I will go back to work for Herrera tomorrow because it is the right thing to do."

"And that's a good reason I suppose," Rosa said.

"It will only be for a week or so and then I can go back to work for Stanley…or maybe for another roofing company that is not as bad to people as Herrera is. I wish I could say Herrera is the only one like that but I cannot. There are others just as bad."

"It's a shame."

"But it's true. And yet there are a few good companies to work for. But they have workers who never want to leave because they pay very well. So it is difficult to get on with one of those companies. I'm always listening to hear if something might come open at a good place but you rarely hear of many new jobs there."

"You know, Armando, I've been thinking. Summer school for Carlos and Maria will be over soon and—what do you think—maybe we could make a trip down to Mexico?"

Armando considered the idea. "It's worth a thought. Where would we go? It has been a long time since we were in Mexico."

"Since Carlos and Maria were very young. I don't think they remember much."

"I don't have family in Saltillo anymore, and anyway that's not where I would prefer to go."

"It's just a thought. We do not have to plan it right now."

Armando nodded slowly. "I can't think about anything right now. My thoughts are filled with the tragedy of the day."

Armando returned to work the next day as he said he would. And the next day as well and all the rest of the week. By Friday afternoon the job was nearly finished. Everyone stayed until past six o'clock to make sure the job was completed so they would not have to come on Saturday to work for Herrera.

When the last shingle was stapled onto the roof everyone climbed down and loaded the equipment into Herrera's truck. Herrera took out his checkbook and slowly and begrudgingly as though it was great pain to do so began writing checks.

"See how lucky you are, you wetbacks," he said and laughed so hard his large belly shook. "Ha, you made money for doing almost nothing this week."

And yet it had been a very difficult week. The roof was a challenge, the temperature was hot as a furnace and one afternoon the sky opened and rain poured down in sheets as gusts of strong wind kicked up making the work even more dangerous.

When Armando looked at the check Herrera had handed him he realized it was fifty dollars less than what Herrera had agreed to pay for the week. Armando was very angry. He wanted to demand that Herrera pay what he said he would but he knew that Herrera was doing this out of spite, maybe hoping that one of the workers would complain. And then Herrera would lunge forward and grab the check and tear it to pieces and there would not be a penny for that man.

All the workers knew this. No one uttered a

word. They clenched their jaw or looked away in anger and quickly folded the check and placed it in their wallet. They could not wait to leave.

As Armando walked to his car one of the older workers came up to him and said, "Did you hear? Towne Roofing is looking for a couple of people for next week. I got a call a little while ago."

Armando's eyes lit. "Towne? The one owned by the Doyle brothers? Billie and Charlie?"

"Yes."

Armando knew it was one of the most decent and best companies to work for, though it was hard to get on with them. Once several years ago Armando had worked briefly for Towne Roofing. They had many good policies and they treated their workers with respect and they paid well and always honored their commitments.

"I have signed on for next week," the man told Armando. He wrote down the phone number of the company and handed it to Armando. "It is a good company, not at all like Herrera. Give them a call. They may still need people."

Armando was grateful. He shook the man's hand and thanked him for the information. "I will call as soon as I get in my car," Armando said. He wasted no time dialing the number. A man at the company gave Armando an address in a part of Houston called Meyerland and told him to be there at eight o'clock on Monday.

When Armando got home he gave Rosa a hug and a kiss and promptly told her the good news about Towne Roofing. Rosa knew he had worked for them in the past and that it was a very good company.

At dinner that evening Rosa asked Carlos and Maria if they would like to go to Mexico later in the summer.

"You will be able to see where your families came from," Rosa said.

"Oh, this is wonderful, Mama," Maria said

beaming brightly. "When will we go?"

"We'll see. I will have to take time off from the hospital. Your father will need to take time off also."

"Why have we never gone before?" Carlos asked.

"Because sometimes it can be difficult to visit one's past. Not that there was anything wrong with it," Armando said. "But when you leave your past behind it is sometimes better that way."

"Will we go to Saltillo where you grew up and where you used to work, Papa?" Carlos asked.

"I don't know," Armando said. "Maybe."

"Oh, I hope we can," Carlos said. "Sometimes at night when I'm lying in bed I imagine that I am working in one of the tile factories like you did. That's funny, isn't it, because I have never been there and don't know what it's like to do that…to work in a tile factory. I imagine I am placing the tiles in the ovens to heat until they are baked hard as rocks."

Armando smiled. "Well, it is very difficult work for a boy. *And* very hot, yes, because the oven gives off much heat that fills the room," Armando explained.

"But it is what you did, isn't it? You worked with the tiles and the ovens?"

"Yes, when I was about your age I did. But then, as you know, I came here and married the most wonderful woman in the whole world. See how your luck can change for the better. See how life can make everything almost perfect?"

"I hope we can go to Mexico," Carlos implored.

"Perhaps we can…we'll see," Rosa said.

"Oh, let's go," Maria pushed. She looked upward and held her hands together. "I pray we can go."

Rosa chuckled. "Yes, we will try. We will try. Now eat your dinner or it will get cold."

"I don't think I can eat," Maria said gently. She put her hands together and looked up again.

"You need lots of energy to think with at school tomorrow," Armando said.

"Yes, Papa, yes. But now I am so happy."

7

Armando drove up to the house where Towne Roofing would be working. He recognized two of the workers. The house was a large forty-year-old place badly in need of new shingles.

As equipment was unloaded from the trucks, Charlie Doyle said, "There she is. A big house and a big job and it will take quite a few days to get it done. Everyone will pay attention to Marco…he is in charge here. He is your boss. Whatever Marco says, goes. And we will pay attention to our rules for the job. They are the same at every job we do and this one is no different. First, every hour is divided into two parts. Fifty minutes on the roof. Ten minutes down in the shade. Lots and lots of water. Everyone wears a harness. Nobody gets on the roof without a harness. I know most companies do not do this but *we* do. We won't have anyone sliding off the roof."

Billie Doyle added, "You'll strip the roof all the way down, old plywood and all. New plywood, new tarpaper, new shingles. There is plenty of plastic. If it rains get it over the top right away. Same at the end of the day. Cover it completely. Marco knows all about it."

The day went smoothly. Every step along the way was controlled precisely by Marco. Towne Roofing stood out from the rest in the way it treated its workers, and the Doyle brothers were proud of this. They paid well and in return they got loyalty and dedication from the workers.

The old shingles were stripped off and by five o'clock part of the rotted plywood had been removed. Armando felt good as he drove home. He wished every job he worked on could be like this one. Even when he worked for Stanley Jarkowski—whose company was one of the more decent ones except for those days when he cut the crew with little notice—even then Stanley was usually fair to his workers. Armando often felt that there was something in Stanley's past, his family's immigrant roots from Eastern Europe perhaps that brought a dose of decency to his company. Armando liked to think that's how it was, anyway.

When Armando arrived home Rosa could tell he was in good spirits and she knew it was probably because of his day working for Towne Roofing.

"So I can see you had a good day," she said to Armando when he came to the kitchen after getting cleaned up. "I am happy because when you have a good day I have a good day. And when you have a bad day I have a bad day."

"Yes. It makes a lot of difference who you work for," Armando said fetching a pitcher of cold water from the refrigerator. "All the workers are in a good mood. They laugh and joke when they are on the roof. And they listen to Mexican music and sing along with it and that makes everyone feel good. Billie and Charlie Doyle are nice people. They expect much from their workers but they do not treat them badly or put unreal demands on them. This time of year being up on the roof for long hours can be dangerous. But Marco sees to it that the whole crew is on the ground once every hour."

"It should be required."

"It should but of course it isn't. Owners like Herrera and many others, even Stanley Jarkowski, would never consider it. And Stanley is better than most…usually. Just last week we heard about someone at another job who had to be taken to the hospital because of heat stroke. He was a young man. The day was terribly hot. He fainted on the roof and they lowered him down and got him to the emergency room."

"Oh, it is very dangerous when that happens. I've seen many brought to the hospital who had been working out in the heat all day. Digging ditches or putting sod on the ground or putting shingles on rooftops, of course. It is very, very dangerous because your heart can stop if your blood pressure drops quickly. Oh my. We need to treat them immediately. We start an IV quickly to get fluid back into their body. Oh, I worry so much about that when you are on the roof on such a hot day like today."

"I will be all right. I always drink lots of water because as fast as you drink it you sweat it off. I am very careful."

"I hope so, Papa!" Maria said, coming into the kitchen while her father was talking.

"You don't need to worry, button, because I am always very careful at work."

Maria hugged her father.

"Now tell me about summer school," Armando said.

Maria went through everything they had done in class and she told him about a test that she got an A on. "And tonight I will write an essay, a one-page report, about a book we read. The book is by a very famous writer named Toni Morrison. I enjoyed every word of it. She tells such a good story. You almost feel like you are right there in the book with the people. Those are the kinds of books I like to read most of all. Toni Morrison was such a good writer that she got a Nobel Prize. Only one person gets that every year. One person out of all the writers in the world. So you can tell how good her writing is just from that."

"Does this now mean that you want to be a writer someday…like the person who wrote the book you just described?"

"Oh no, Papa! I still want to be a doctor…a surgeon. But I will continue to read all the time.

At night when I am not at the hospital taking care of people I will read lots of books."

"Now go call your brother and we will eat," Rosa said.

⅄

Armando was glad to return to work at Towne Roofing the next day. By eleven o'clock the old plywood had been removed. New sheets were cut on the ground to the exact size and raised to the roof and nailed in place. Everything was co-ordinated perfectly.

Lunch at midday was forty-five minutes in the shade of a large tree and then everyone talked about their children or about the big red snapper they claimed they caught last week in the gulf and then they climbed to the roof again and re-turned to their assigned jobs.

Before going up the workers hooked their harnesses tightly to the tether attached to the roof. Although it was yet one more piece of heavy and hot clothing the benefit was obvious to everyone.

All the workers but Armando and Marco had climbed the ladder. Armando started up. He was almost to the top when his foot slipped off a rung. He tumbled down and as he reached for a rung he twisted his shoulder.

"Armando!" Marco yelled, racing over.

The tethered harness had buffered the fall but not enough to prevent Armando's shoulder from turning.

"Armando, Armando, are you okay?" Marco said as he crouched next to him on the ground.

Armando was breathing deep.

"Don't move...you might hurt yourself more." Marco called up to the roof. "Francisco, come here quickly! Quickly, Francisco! Quickly!"

Francisco scurried to the ladder and lowered himself down.

"What do you think, Armando?" Marco said. "Do you think you have broken it?"

Armando's eyes glazed over. He shook his head slowly. "I don't know."

"We'll get you to the hospital. Thank God we are near the Medical Center. We'll get you over there immediately. Can you stand up?"

"Yes, I think so."

"Slowly," Marco told Francisco. "Take his other arm…very gently. Put it over your shoulder. I'll guide this side. We will go in your truck to the emergency room at Hermann Hospital. It's not far away. We can be there in no time. Don't move your arm, Armando. I'll hold it still."

Francisco drove to the hospital. Marco called Billie Doyle and explained what had happened. He said he would meet them at the hospital.

When they arrived at the hospital, Marco got a wheelchair for Armando; they rolled him into the emergency room. The waiting room was packed with people with hands and arms and heads wrapped in makeshift bandages. Worried families paced nervously. Doctors and nurses came and went in and out of the treatment area.

"Do you want me to get in touch with any-one, Armando?"

"Yes." He pulled his phone from his pocket and with his thumb scrolled down to Rosa's phone number. "Here, punch this in for me if you will."

Marco handed the phone to Armando.

"Armando?" Rosa said.

"Hi, love," he moaned. He pulled in a deep breath and said, "I'm over at Hermann in the ER. I slipped down the ladder and twisted my arm. My elbow and shoulder are...well, I don't know...."

"Oh, no, no! I'm on my way. I'm here at Methodist just two blocks away. I'll be right there. Don't go anywhere."

Armando laughed a little. He looked at Marco. "My wife will be here in a minute. She works down the street."

Rosa rushed into the ER. "Oh, *Armando*," she said. "What *happened*?"

Armando described how he slipped from the top of the ladder. He told her he was going up the ladder after the lunch break and how the Doyle brothers allowed everyone to take a long rest and how it makes you ready to return to the job again.

Rosa nodded. She knew the days of summer were hot and she worried about that for Armando and the other workers who endured the scorching heat of the roof.

"He had on his harness. It prevented him from crashing to the ground," Marco said. "But he twisted his arm on the way down."

A nurse examined Armando's arm. "We will try to get to you as soon as we can. As you can see, we are packed with patients today…just like every day. But we'll do the best we can. I won't be able to give you anything for pain until the doctor sees you first."

Armando nodded. "I will be okay."

A short while later Billie Doyle rushed in.

"This is Armando Ortiz," Marco said.

"Yes, I remember," Billie replied.

Marco explained what happened.

"You have not seen a doctor yet, I gather," Billie said.

"No, not yet," Marco said. "From the looks of things, it may be quite a while."

"Uh-huh, yes," Billie Doyle said. He went to the reception desk. When he came back, he said, "I gave them the credit card number for the company. We will cover whatever charges there are for the ER." He opened his wallet. "Well, Armando, you will not be able to work any-more this week, I suspect. So he's a hundred dollars for the lost time." He pulled a second hundred-dollar bill out. "And here is a little extra. I have to go now. But take care, Armando, and get better quickly. I think you are in good hands here." He gave an encouraging smile and started to leave, then turned and looked back. "Thank God for the harness!"

After Billie Doyle left, Rosa looked at Marco and said, "You don't need to stay. I'll be with Armando today. Oh, thank you so much for getting him over here."

Marco nodded and smiled and left with Francisco to return to work.

By three o'clock, Armando seemed no further along in his wait for treatment than when he came in at noon. The room was more crowded than ever; the odor of people overtook the calm ambiance of the waiting area. One after another, ambulances whistled up to the large emergency room doors and people were brought in. Some looked very sick and others, like Armando, were merely in need of treatment.

Armando closed his eyes and sat patiently. "Maybe you should go home, love," he told Rosa. "I think I am going to be here for quite a while. Maybe until later this evening."

"Oh, Armando, don't be silly. I would never

leave you here. And anyway, I will need to know what the doctor says."

It was almost five hours before Armando was finally examined. His shoulder and elbow were X-rayed. Eventually a resident stopped by the bay where Armando was lying.

"From what I can tell you didn't break anything. It may not feel like it but you didn't. We will need to have one of the orthopedic surgeons look at the X-ray. I don't know when that will be. Not too long, I hope. One of them is seeing another patient now. I'll try to get him over to take a look and talk with you. Just a little longer."

The surgeon eventually came over and confirmed that there were no broken bones. "Bruised muscles and ligaments probably," he said. "You will be sore for quite a few days. You need to give the shoulder a rest. We will give you a sling. It will help and will let everything heal. But you need to move the arm and elbow each day…several times like this." He showed Armando what to do. "If you don't do that the shoulder will become very stiff…a frozen shoulder is what we call it. You don't want that. I will give you some medication to take with you and a prescription to keep the swelling down. Do you have a doctor you can see for a follow up?"

"Yes," Rosa replied.

"So take care of your arm and stay off roofs for a week or so." He shook Armando's hand and headed off to see another patient.

Armando and Rosa got home late that evening. Maria and Carlos were waiting nervously for them. They each gave a big hug to their father around his waist.

"Oh Papa, what happened to you?" Maria asked.

Carlos and Maria listened wide-eyed as Armando explained. To Carlos, his father was the strongest and bravest man he had ever known.

Nothing could hurt his father, that's what he believed. He knew that as a boy he had worked in the tile factories and that he was able to bring home money to support his mother and the family. That made him proud of his father. And he knew that every day he climbed onto steep roofs and stapled shingles onto them. And that made him even more proud of his father. In Carlos's eyes he was someone that no harm would ever come to.

Rosa said, "Now I want your Papa to sit in a comfortable chair in the living room and rest. I will get him a bite to eat. And something for the two of you as well. I'm sure you are both hungry."

"Oh Mama, I was too worried to be hungry," Maria said.

"Yes, but now everything will be fine. You need to eat," Armando said. "I am going to rest for a while. The doctor gave me something for pain at the hospital. It is helping already."

Armando sat in his favorite soft chair. Rosa arranged his sling comfortably next to him.

"See how lucky we are to have someone like your mother who knows all about this," Armando said to Carlos and Maria. He rested his head back on the cushion. "And the people at the hospital were very good. It was very busy but they were patient with everyone."

Rosa said, "In an emergency room there are always people who are extremely sick when they come in. The nurses and doctors must take care of them first." Rosa looked at Maria and said, "Someday when you are a doctor you will learn all about it."

After Carlos and Maria had dinner, Rosa told them they needed to get some rest. It had been a long day and they had classes in the morning.

Rosa and Armando sat in the living room with the lights turned down low. Armando said, "Rosa, my dear, I think you should get some sleep too. Waiting for so many hours in the emergency room was very tiring."

"I wanted to be with you at the hospital."

"Well anyway, I think I'll just sit here quietly by myself."

"Yes…if you'd like. When you come to bed, I will put your arm in a comfortable position so you don't lay on it. And tomorrow we will do the exercises the doctor showed us." She gave Armando a kiss and said if he needed anything to call out; she would be able to hear him.

Armando sat in the dim light. He closed his eyes and thought about the day. How could he have slipped off the ladder? In all his days as a roofer he had never done that, had hardly ever slipped on the roof, even a little. Thinking about it bothered him. He had hoped that Marco might put in a good word with the Doyle brothers and that he might become a permanent member of their team. Nothing would make him happier than to work for them every day.

But now he knew that would never happen. Armando felt old. He felt like he was too old to be up on the roof. He knew that Rosa worried about it all the time. Most of the other workers around him were younger. Many companies wanted them because they could zip around quickly on the roof and because they worked very hard. People like Herrera always chose young men because they were the easiest of all to cheat. They never complained. They accepted all the guff Herrera dished out and never said a word.

Maybe this is a good time for me to get serious about starting my own company, Armando thought. *Time to stop imagining and finally do whatever needs to be done.* He thought about what his mother had told him when he was young. She would say, "Armando, when something unpleasant happens try to find some good in it." He closed his eyes, he could hear his mother's words.

Yes, I will do that, he told himself. *I will look for the good in this even though it is hard to imagine that there is any.* And just as if she were now speaking to him he could hear her say, "Try, Armando. You might be surprised."

Armando thought, *All right I will try. Who knows? I may be surprised. But what good could there be in the danger and trouble that came to me today? What? I have already given it much thought. When I was in the emergency room at the hospital, I thought about it. I would never tell Rosa my worries because I know what she would say. She would say, 'Oh Armando, God will make sure you are okay'.* Armando laughed a little because he could always predict what she would tell him. He always knew what she would say. He liked that about being married to her and he wondered if all married people were like that.

He thought about his children as he frequently did when he was sitting in the living room late at night by himself. He hoped they would be accepted in America. And yet he knew there were times when they were not. He knew Rosa had heard the stories about how another boy or girl at school chided and taunted them. Armando knew what it was like because it happened to him when he came from Mexico. Even Rosa had experienced it and yet she was born in the US. But most of all he hoped his children's dreams would come true. That Maria would become a doctor as she hoped to be. And that Carlos would become a Senator for the State of Texas. Armando chuckled at the thought of that and it made him forget about his shoulder.

8

Armando let his shoulder heal as he was told to do in the ER. He and Rosa made a visit to a doctor Rosa knew from the hospital. Rosa liked him because he always spent time talking to his patients. He discussed their medical problems in detail and had a soft and gentle way of dealing with people.

But now Rosa was worried more than ever about Armando going back onto the roofs. She thought his strength and balance might not be as good as when he was younger. She did not tell him this because it would only worry him more. So she did not mention it to him even though the thought of it continued to bother her.

Armando's shoulder felt much better though he knew it was not as it had been before he fell. It was stiff and didn't move as smoothly, but he did not tell Rosa this.

Ten days after the accident he said to Rosa, "I feel very good, my love. My shoulder is better than when I was a young man." Rosa smiled and when she did Armando knew she did not believe him and that it was her gentle way of letting him know.

"I would like to work again for the Doyle brothers," Armando said as he sat in the kitchen with her.

"If you have to go up on the roof…I suppose," Rosa conceded reluctantly.

"They are fair and they always treat their people well. Never would any of the other companies have done what Billie Doyle did the day I twisted my arm."

"You were very lucky." Rosa put her hands together. "See…some days even when life takes a bad turn God helps us."

"But the Doyle brothers will never take me back. This much I'm sure of. They will not want to hire an old roofer like me when they can get young men who never slip and who go across the roof without fear," Armando said. "Perhaps when we get older we start to think of bad things that can happen to us."

"Maybe it's smart that we do, Armando. Maybe it is," Rosa said.

Armando agreed. If nothing more, it told him that he was worried about it. He knew the roofs were dangerous, just as Rosa knew. He knew that Rosa wanted him to do some other kind of work. Even construction. If it was inside work it would be much safer. But he had worked in construction only briefly when he first came to the States.

In the morning Armando called Marco to see if there was work for him at Towne Roofing. He decided to try; he had nothing to lose. Marco might pretend there was no work if he knew Billie Doyle did not want to hire him after his fall. Or it was possible that they had no openings and that would be the end of it for now.

"What do you think?" Armando said to Marco. "Is there a chance I can get back with Towne Roofing? Nothing would make me happier."

"You just might be in luck, amigo. Billie is looking for two people right now. How is your shoulder? I guess that's the question."

"It is much better. Like normal. I am grateful to you and Francisco for getting me quickly to the hospital."

"I will check with Billie and get back to you. I know he needs people for today."

"Yes, please," Armando replied quickly.

Marco called back within minutes. "It's okay with Billie. Today we are working over in Sharpstown. Can you make it?"

"I'll be there. I'll be there," Armando eagerly replied.

Armando had a good day working for Towne Roofing despite the mid-summer heat. Billie Doyle assigned Armando to work on the ground and kept him off the roof, though he did not have to do that, but he liked Armando and was happy to have him rejoin the crew. He could tell Armando had a strong work ethic and that's what mattered to the Doyle brothers most of all. They selected their workers as much as possible based on that. And in return all the workers were happy to be part of the group. Many of them could have worked elsewhere—even in construction jobs, safer jobs, jobs that were less demanding on the body, jobs that did not expose them to the extreme heat of the summer and the cold of the winter but they preferred to stay with the Doyle brothers. No one complained that Billie Doyle had gone easy on Armando when he came back because they knew Billie would have done the same for them. They respected the Doyle brothers and the Doyle brothers respected them.

On his third day on the job Armando decided to talk to Billie Doyle about something he had been wanting to ask for a long time but did not have the courage until now.

Wednesday at noon Billie Doyle came by to see how the job was going. He talked to the crew as they sat on the ground on their lunch break. When Billie started back to his truck Armando followed him.

"Excuse me, Mr. Doyle," Armando said. "I want to express my thanks for what you did when I twisted my arm."

Billie Doyle smiled and said, "It's part of our job as an employer. You see, me and Charlie had a company up in Boston. We worked all around the city and in the suburbs. But we wanted to get away from the cold and snow so we came down here where it never snows but where the heat fries you like one of those jumbo shrimps when you're up on the roof." He laughed with great gusto.

"Can I ask you a question, Mr. Doyle?"

"Only if you quit calling me Mr. Doyle and start calling me Billie."

Armando nodded. "Well, I have a rather unusual question but it would be very kind of you if you would tell me what you think."

"Shoot," Billie Doyle said.

Armando pulled in a breath. "You will probably fire me but I'll ask anyway."

Billie Doyle waited.

Armando said, "Okay, here goes. See I've worked on the roof for many years. I shouldn't tell you how many or you'll think I am an old man."

A kind grin came to Billie Doyle's face.

"Okay, here goes," Armando said again. "Well…I've been thinking about starting my own roofing company. I know I shouldn't tell you this because you will probably fire me right away. Well, I'm wondering if you could…if you would tell me how you got started. I've talked with my wife, Rosa, many times about this. But all we do is talk about it. Now I think it is time to do it."

Billie granted Armando a warm smile. He said, "You may need to make a few purchases. A truck, if you do not have one. Maybe two trucks. Some good ladders. And do not forget the harnesses. Do not do this if you are not going to buy harnesses. But even with that you need to have insurance. Insurance that will cover your workers. Insurance that will cover the job itself. No matter how much you try to make the job a good one there will be people who will say you did not do it right."

"I am glad to hear all this," Armando said. "And I will never take work from you…if and when I start my own company. I will never—"

Billie Doyle chuckled. "I'm going to let you

in on a little secret, my friend. Most of the roofing companies will think you are trying to take
work from them or that you are trying to steal
their workers. It happens to me all the time. But
here is the secret." Billie Doyle talked in a
hushed voice as if he thought someone would
hear. "Guess what, Armando? There are more
houses in Houston than there are roofers." And
Billie Doyle let out a laugh so brisk his band of
workers on the ground under the tree looked
over. "Yes, it is true. There are more houses in
Houston than there are roofing companies. So,
you see, I have no worries that you will steal jobs
from me. I can't keep up with the jobs we have."

Armando's joy was proof that what his
mother had told him years ago was true: you
must let your dreams lead you. If you do not, you
will never live to fulfill them. When you have a
dream make it more than a dream. Make it part
of your life. Make it come true.

Armando thanked Billie Doyle. He had

given Armando the courage to act on his dream.

Billie Doyle nodded and climbed into his truck. "Now I have another job to check on," he said. "And don't forget to talk this over with the bank."

Armando returned to the others sitting under the tree on their lunch break. One of them said, "So you want to start your own company?"

Armando did not lie to them. "It would be good, I think," he replied. "I would like to."

"I would like to also," one of the workers said. "But my English is no good. I cannot speak no good and it would be useless. I see how the roofing company owners must get good with the house owner. Even people like Herrera who is a sonuvabitch, and we know it is true because we have all worked for him on those days when it is either that or sit under the bridge for someone to come by and get us for work. And maybe no one picks us. And even then sometimes we get cheated. Then, I wish I could start my own company. But my English is no good."

"When you start a company, can we work for you?" another worker asked. "I think you will be fair like the Doyle brothers are. I think so. Of course, I would never leave them. They have been good to me. I would never leave them."

"The Doyle brother are good…good and fair and that is the most important thing of all," Armando said.

When Armando returned home that afternoon, Rosa could tell he was in a very good mood, that he was especially happy. It might have been from just being able to work for Billie and Charlie Doyle but she was sure there was more to it than that.

After Armando got cleaned up he came down and sat in the kitchen as Rosa was making dinner.

"I have some wonderful news to tell you," he said. "I talked with Billie Doyle today about starting my own company."

Rosa stopped cooking and looked at Armando as if wondering whether it was a wise thing to do.

"Don't worry, love, everything went well…went very well in fact. Billie Doyle is a good man. I know I took a risk talking to him but I felt it was necessary." Armando knew Rosa would approve because they always thought alike, and he believed that marriage brings people together in a unique unscripted sort of way. He knew if he had told her what he was planning to do she would have smiled and said, "I am always with you, Armando, my dear. Always, always, always." She had said it to him a thousand times.

"Billie Doyle gave me a lot of good advice but most of all I was convinced that what I want to do…what *we* want to do, you and me, is not unrealistic. When you get advice from someone like Billie Doyle you feel that it is believable and right."

Armando got up and went to the refrigerator and retrieved a can of Modelo beer. "And now I will give myself a little treat," he said, flipping the tab and watching the foam bubble silently across the top. "What about you, my dear? Can I get a Modelo for you? This is a big occasion, I think."

"Oh, no thank you. But I am glad you are happy. Just seeing you happy makes me happy too."

"Remember years ago when we first met? The evening we went to the dance at St. Michaels—"

"Yes, how could I forget?"

"And afterwards when we were talking I said I wanted someday to own my own company because I believed it was possible in America? Remember? That it was the American dream to do so. All my life…all my life I believed in the American dream."

"Yes, I remember," Rosa said fondly.

"Well, now is my chance." Armando's voice was full of confidence. "And here we are many years later and I feel so sure, so…what should I say? So determined to make it all happen."

"I know you will."

"Maybe this week I will stop in at the bank and talk to them. Perhaps we should go together. It will be better if we are both there together."

"Well, you probably should go because I don't know anything about business or banking or about roofing companies."

Armando laughed. "Well, I don't know anything about banking and not much about business but I do know a lot about roofing companies. That might be a start."

Dinner was joyful that night. Maria and Carlos told Armando what they learned that day…what they learned in school and what they learned about life. Rosa mentioned again the possibility of going to Mexico for a visit after summer school was out.

"Oh, please, Mama, let's go," Maria bubbled.

"Yes, yes, please. Let's go," Carlos said.

Now Rosa knew she was stuck…she could not say no.

9

On Saturday Armando went to one of the local banks. Rosa went along but waited in the car. Armando knew she would be saying a prayer for him. Armando was dressed in his best clothes for the occasion—clothes he wore to Mass on Sundays with the family. A suit, a starched shirt, and a handsome tie. He owned only one suit but it was a nice suit nonetheless and it still looked almost new. Armando, if lean, looked healthy for his age. He often said, "I sweat out every ounce of fat in my body every day on the roof."

Armando thought his visit went well. A young banker named Burkhart listened carefully to Armando's plans. Burkhart seemed pleased with Armando's presentation. He had planned everything to the letter—the costs of every part of it. They talked about the insurance, which the bank would require if they were to loan Armando the money for two vans, ladders, harnesses, shingles, plywood, and tarpaper, all until he could afford it on his own. He knew the costs, had checked to find and tally how much they would be. He did not want to appear unprepared, to be unfamiliar with the complexities of running his own company.

He felt very confident when he came out to the car. He was not used to speaking with bankers and he worried that his accent might prejudice their opinions and turn them against him. He knew this could happen. Some bankers, like many other business people, were good at hiding their prejudices. They had learned how to masquerade their true feelings. He worried that the bankers might fear that too many Hispanics were already in the roofing business. Despite the risk associated with running a roofing company, much money was to be made even from a smaller one. And of course even more so by the companies that could work two, three, maybe four jobs at once. Companies like the one Herrera owned. Many of the banks limited the number of loans they gave to companies owned by Hispanics; they did not like having too many enterprises in the hands of Latinos and Hispanics. Armando knew this to be true.

Even though Rosa wasn't with him in the bank she felt that he had done well. She was always his support team in everything about life. And of course this made life easier for Armando. Even he doubted his own abilities now and then. It was hard not to sometimes, life being as difficult and troubling as it often was.

"And now we just have to wait to hear what they say," Armando said, as he sat in the car.

"Perhaps it's a good time to take Carlos and

Maria to Mexico like we promised."

Armando thought it over. "Better to wait until we hear from the bank. I don't think it will take long."

On Monday Armando again got a call from Marco saying Billie Doyle wanted to know if Armando was available to work. Armando was amazed. He still believed he would never get requests from the Doyle brothers to join their group after his fall from the ladder.

Armando was anxious to join the group. He said he could leave right away and be at the worksite soon. Marco was there when Armando pulled up. Soon the others arrived. Billie Doyle parked his van in front of the house. He gave the crew the usual instructions. Afterward, he came over to Armando.

"Have you given more thought to starting a company?" Billie Doyle asked. "Remember what I told you, there are more houses in Houston than there are roofers." A big Irish smile filled his face.

"Yes. I went to the bank and talked to one of the bankers in the loan department for quite a while. I think they believed I could do it and that my company would succeed. I am not looking for a great deal of money, and any-way, I have collateral for the loan in the form of our house, which we have paid for. So I'm hoping all will go well."

Billie Doyle shook Armando's hand and wished him luck. As he was leaving, he called to the workers, "Remember, lots of water. Lots and lots of water." He looked at Marco and said, "Make sure they do. It's too damn hot up there," he said, pointing up with his thumb. "Let's not have any heatstroke."

The morning and afternoon went well. Armando felt as though his shoulder was almost completely healed. He was sure he could keep pace with the other workers. Three times before lunch and four times afterward the crew was on the ground for ten minutes in the shade. Marco saw to it that they adhered to Billie Doyle's hard and fast rule about it. The temperature of the day soared. By mid-afternoon the heat bearing down on the roof made the metal tools almost too hot to handle.

Armando was glad to be working for Billie Doyle and he wished he could do it as much as possible. Of course, most of all he wanted to start his own company. Almost every evening he talked with Rosa about it, anxiously waiting for the bank to get back to them. It seemed to be taking a long time. He was not sure why that was, but then he knew little about the workings of a bank. Each day he was certain they would get in touch with him and each day passed without a word.

"Do you think I should give them a call? Perhaps they think I wasn't serious," he told Rosa.

"I am very sure they know you are serious.

I am positive of that. They will get back to you any day now. Be patient. After all, they are in the business of loaning money. That's how *they* make *their* money."

"We should own a bank...what do you think? All you do is give people money and charge them interest," Armando joked. "And sit in air-conditioned offices in big leather chairs. Bankers never have to worry about falling off a roof."

"If only we had a couple hundred million dollars," Rosa said. "Then we could do that. Wouldn't it be fun!"

"And what would we call this bank of ours?" Armando asked.

Rosa thought for a minute. She tilted her head, and said, "All right now...let's see...*The Armando and Rosa First State Bank of Tejas.* How does that sound?"

"There you go. We are in the wrong business for sure. But mostly what we will do is see to it that the dreams of people come true."

"I know you, Armando. You will want to give a loan to anyone who asks for it," Rosa said.

"Yes, I am very generous. I admit it," Armando replied with a sign of the cross.

"But what if they don't do what they say they will? What if they go out and buy a big expensive car and drive off and don't repay the loan?" Rosa said.

"See…you are much more practical than I am. I never think about those things. That's why we will make you the president of the bank. We will need to change the name of the bank to *The Rosa and Armando First State Bank of Tejas*.

Armando waited patiently. Another week passed and then at last one day the bank called. They said they would like for Armando to stop by when he had a chance. It turned out that the job with Towne Roofing was scheduled to finish on Thursday. Armando made an appointment with the bank for ten o'clock Friday morning.

Rosa went to bed early Thursday night.

Armando sat in his favorite chair, lights off with only the sparkle of the streetlamp coming in through the window. He felt nervous yet confident about the meeting. If all went well his dream might come true in just a few hours. How many years had he waited? Even before he came to the US. Even as a boy in Saltillo. So many years!

Was the American dream about to come true for him? Was it about to? Could it? The darkness of the room was like a blanket that wrapped around Armando. A soft serape. He felt as though he could touch the softness. Reach out and touch it. He knew that Rosa, the love of his life, and his two children, whom he cherished, were comfortably asleep. That made Armando feel good. And he knew that his mother was with him that night. He could see her smiling ever so delicately in the darkness. And it gave him strength to know he had so many people supporting him. Even the support of the Doyle brothers helped convince Armando his dream would come true. They, too, had once been where he was now and they succeeded. Had in fact become the most decent and truthful roofing company in Houston. That would be the model Armando would follow.

Friday morning was clear and warm when Armando drove to the bank. He wanted to be at the bank on time. As before, Rosa went along. She would wait in the car and say a prayer on Armando's behalf while he was with the bankers.

"Bankers are probably very busy. It must take a lot of time to count all that money," Armando said as they rode along. They laughed and it made Armando relax. He looked at Rosa, winked, and said, "You look wonderful today."

Sitting in the bank, Armando looked frequently at his watch. It seemed like he had been there a long time. *It's like waiting to see the doctor in the ER*, he thought. Time crawled by.

Finally, Burkhart came from his office. He smiled and greeted Armando and seemed in good spirits.

"Ah, good morning," Burkhart said in a jazzy voice. "Come in, let's go over your loan." In the office was another man. Burkhart introduced him and said he was the vice president of the loan department. The man had short hair and a reasonable demeanor. He shook Armando's hand firmly.

Burkhart talked about the weather, how it had been an unusually hot summer, then said, "Well, let's take a look at your loan, shall we?"

He opened a file that was on his desk. A desk that had two computer screens but was otherwise mostly empty.

"We have looked this over very carefully," Burkhart started. "You have good collateral. I think you could repay the loan if you ran into trouble. That is…well, I almost hate to say it this way but it is probably the most important thing to the bank. So I think all is fine in that regard."

Armando nodded and held a smile for a moment. He could tell the bank had studied his application thoroughly. They had more than a week to consider it. The expression on Burkhart's face suggested he would grant Armando the loan. Armando knew that the size of the loan was modest, small even, compared to the huge loans banks often made. A hundred thousand here, a million there. Armando was asking for little more than eighty thousand dollars, top to bottom. Hardly anything. What's more, he could back up the entire loan with collateral from his home. Armando sat quietly. He felt his hand tremble ever so slightly.

Burkhart paged through a small stack of papers, turning them over and going back to the beginning. While he did, he said, "Armando, as a point of interest, how many roofing companies do you think there are in Houston?" The words came out flat and mechanical.

"In Houston? Well, I would have to take a guess," Armando replied, feeling suddenly uncomfortable. "Well, let's see. I've been in the business for a long time. Working as a roofer is what I mean. I've got a good feel for it all," Armando said confidently. "I'd be surprised if there were more than a hundred companies. And even that might be a lot. Probably more like fifty or sixty in all."

"Fifty or sixty. Okay," Burkhart repeated.

"Something like that. Yes."

"Tell you what, we'll go with a hundred, to be on the safe side." Burkhart tilted back in his chair. He put his fingertips together and tapped them in a bankerly sort of way. After a moment he glanced toward the ceiling as if engaged in mental calculations of some sort. "A hundred roofers, okay. Of course, Houston is a big city. A darn big city. I've lost track of the population. Four million, maybe. Something like that. Something. Everywhere you look there's a new house going up…isn't there? Houston has always been a boom town."

Burkhart's fingers slid quickly across a calculator. "Let's just say four million. How's that sound?" he rhetorically asked. "And let's go with a hundred roofers, how's that?" he again said. "That's one roofing company for every forty thousand people." He looked at Armando. "Pretty darn good odds for a roofing company. Darn good odds. But the real challenge in any business is finding work, finding the jobs. A good marketing plan is almost as important as good ladders and vans and shingles."

The vice president took over. "What Mr. Burkhart is saying is that we will need a strong marketing plan. I'm afraid that's the weakness in your application."

"Well, I'm sure I can put one together for you," Armando said, fearing that the application was dead.

"I'm sure you probably can," Burkhart said

with a nod. "They are not so hard to do, especially if you get in touch with someone who knows how to do it. And so, my recommendation is that you go back and start from scratch. I'm afraid we will not be able to help you with a loan."

A cold and bare silence spread through the room as the vice president said, "And perhaps try another bank as well. Just like there are many roofing companies there are also many banks. Perhaps your time here will help you with another bank. We hope so."

Walking across the parking lot, Armando felt as if life had drained from him. He had convinced himself that all would go well and that he would now be able to embark on his dream. He sat in their car and stared quietly downward.

Rosa knew the loan had been denied. "Don't feel so bad, Armando," she said. "It is just one bank. There are many more we can try. I know how much you wanted this but there are still more possibilities."

Armando said nothing. He put the key in the ignition but did not turn on the car. After a long while, he said, "Yes, love, I know you are correct…as you always are at times like this. And I'm grateful for that. But…well. But you know how much I was hoping for a better response from the bank. Now I wonder if maybe it was all a waste of time. You know how I am. I always believe we will succeed."

"Yes, I know you do. And I am happy you do. You believe in yourself and that's important. From the time we met I saw that wonderful quality you have."

Armando nodded. He started the car and headed home.

"I can make a good lunch for us when we get back."

"If you want. But I think I am not so hungry now."

"If I put something on the table, we can all

eat. Carlos and Maria and the two of us. It will make you feel better. I know it will."

Armando smiled as best he could. He felt lucky to have Rosa. He knew she was a true and faithful companion in his journey of life. He knew this almost from the first day they met in Corpus Christi. At moments like this he was especially sure of it.

10

Armando returned to Towne Roofing Monday morning. Though he was still unhappy about the decision of the bank, he was grateful to be working for Billie and Charlie Doyle. August that year was hot and cruel. It delivered vengeful sweltering days from the moment the crew climbed onto the roof. Days that went slowly as though they would never end, even with the chance to get down from the roof and cool off for a few minutes in the shade and drink many cups of water.

Later, when the day was over and the crew was gathering equipment Billie Doyle pulled up in his truck. He talked to Marco for a few minutes and then came over to Armando.

"How did it go with the bank?"

"Not well. They turned down the loan."

"Really. Did they say why?"

Armando explained about the marketing plan.

Billie shook his head. "That's gahbage," he pointedly said in his Boston accent. "Nobody needs a mahketing plan to slap shingles on a roof. Let me tell you what the mahketing plan is: you find a job, you have your people climb on the roof and put on new shingles. *That's* the only mahketing plan you need. What they're telling you is bullshit, that's what it is. Okay, you will have to advertise. I agree with that. But actually that part is pretty simple. And anyway, once you get a few jobs, if the customers are happy they are your best advertisers. I get most of my new jobs from the recommendations of others."

"But now I feel stuck," Armando said. "I'm not so sure what to do."

"Keep going. Try another bank. And others, too, if you have to. You might get lucky. Don't get discouraged, amigo. Okay? Keep at it."

Driving home, Armando felt better having talked to Billie Doyle. He always had a way of making everything seem simple even when they were working on an especially difficult job.

Armando turned down Hillcroft Road and onto Bellaire Boulevard heading toward the Hispanic neighborhoods of west Houston, the enclaves of Houston's working middle-class. People who were happy to do any kind of work. Men with calloused hands and women returning from domestic work and cleaning jobs throughout the city.

Armando looked into his mirror and noticed a police car. It had just turned off a side street and was following him closely.

"Ah, no!" he mumbled. He glanced at the speedometer. Barely forty and no faster than the others cars around him. He watched the patrol car as it moved down the road a few feet behind him. Why had Armando been singled out? Yet, he knew these things happened randomly for no reason at all. Perhaps the police would turn at the corner or swing into the other lane and ignore him. Two cars passed Armando in the lane to his left. *There*, he thought, *the police cannot be after me. Look at all the others zoom by.*

Armando pulled to a stop light, waited for the light to change, and started forward, the police car still behind him. Before he had gone twenty feet a row of blue lights flashed on top of the car. Armando came to a stop on the side of the road.

The police officer came up to the car and asked to see Armando's driver license and insurance card. He looked at them carefully and glanced at Armando almost suspiciously.

"Where you are going, compadre?" the officer said, still holding the documents.

"Home, sir. I just got off work."

"Hmm. Where was that?"

"In Meyerland, sir. I work for a roofing company. We're doing a job there."

"Roofing, huh?"

"Yes, sir."

"Roofing, huh?"

"Yes, sir. Towne Roofing company."

"All right. Are you aware you have a brake light out?"

"Oh, no. I didn't know."

"Well, you do. On the right side. Need to get it fixed."

"Yes, sir. Yes, sir. I will. Right away."

"I'm not going to write you a ticket. Get it fixed, okay?"

"Thank you."

What more can go wrong today? Armando thought as he pulled into the driveway.

He washed his hands in the kitchen and sat at the table. He told Rosa about the car and started to tell her about his conversation with

Billie Doyle when she said, "First, I think you should talk to Carlos. He has something to show you."

"I've got to get cleaned up. It was a miserable hot day today. I'll talk to him."

Armando took a shower and put on clean clothes and went to Carlos's room. The door was closed. Armando tapped gently on it. He got no reply. He nudged the door open. Carlos was working at his desk, his back to Armando.

"Hey, buddy, what's up?"

"Doing homework, Papa." His back still to Armando.

"I was told you have something to show me."

No reply.

"Well?"

Still no reply.

"Car…los," Armando said, sympathetically. "What's up, buddy?"

Finally, Carlos turned and looked at his father. Face cast down. A bright purple half-moon hung below his left eye.

"Hmm. Now that is indeed a surprise, my boy," Armando uttered. "Hmm." Armando sat on the bed. "Come over here and tell me what happened."

Carlos shuffled over and sat hunched next to his father.

"Now how did you get that?"

Carlos stared straight ahead, saying nothing for a moment, then said, "He called me a name. A bad name."

"Who did?"

"A kid at school."

What did he say?

"He called me a wetback."

"And?"

"I told him to shut up and I started to walk away like you always told me to do."

"And then?"

"He did it again. And then he called me another name."

"And what did you do?"

"I told him to stop it. He pushed me and I fell over onto the ground. I was very mad but he was bigger than me. When I got up he called me a name again…not a wetback but a worse name and then he tried to punch me but I moved and he hit my shoulder. I told him to stop but he hit me again and this time I swung and hit him with my fist. I don't think I hit him very hard but it made him real mad and he gave me a big hit on my face."

"Look here. Let me see where." Armando examined the bruise closely. "I think it will be all right. From what I can tell your eye seems fine. The bruise may be there for a couple of days, I suppose."

"I don't want to go downstairs. Maria might laugh or something."

"I know she won't, Carlos. Maria is a very

sensitive person. Please…come down. Mama is making tacos, and I know you love her tacos."

For a moment, at least, Carlos's eye did not hurt as much.

Armando went to the kitchen. "Yes, that was quite a surprise. Did you talk with him?" he asked Rosa.

"Oh, of course. I told him these kinds of things will happen from time to time and he must not let them bother him too much. I explained that it even happened to me when I was growing up in Corpus Christi. I told Carlos he does not have to worry about anything because he was born here and has as much right to be in America as anyone. In fact, I was born here and now he and Maria were born here, too. So that makes them second generation Americans. This is where we live. It is our home. He seemed to appreciate it when I told him that. I think he will be okay."

"Quite a shiner, he has," Armando said, sitting at the kitchen table.

"I looked it over carefully. I think he will be okay. Now my dear esposo, tell me some good news. That's what I need right now. Some good news from my sweetheart," Rosa said.

"Okay, well…I talked with Billie Doyle at work today after we were done. I told him about the bank and he said not to let that bother me. He said I should go to another bank."

Rosa stopped cooking and looked at Armando. "See, just like I said."

"Yes, you did. I should know after all these years to listen to you. And just like you, Billie Doyle said there are many banks in Houston. One of them will give us a loan and then we can start a company of our own." Armando leaned back in the chair and looked at the ceiling. "Now…what will we call it? Hmm, now what would be a good name for this wonderful company we will start?"

Barely a second passed when Rosa said, "Perfect Roofing."

"Wow…and what made you think of that?"

"I don't know. It just suddenly leaped into my mind," Rosa replied as she placed tortillas in a pan to warm.

"Perfect Roofing," Armando said, slowly and thoughtfully. "I think that is a very good name…Perfect Roofing. And yes, it will be a perfect roofing company. It will be perfect for the customers and perfect for the people who work there. And of course it will be perfect for us—for the whole family."

Dinner was a simple meal of tacos and refritos and Carlos did not need coaxing to come down for dinner. No one made a comment about his purple eye.

"Mama, I thought we were going to take a trip to Mexico when summer school was over," Maria said.

"Yes, we talked about it. But unfortunately

we will not be able to make it now, sweetheart. Your father is very busy getting a loan to start a company," Rosa said.

"Oh…I'm very disappointed. I was hoping so much we would go," Maria said.

"So was I," Carlos said.

"We will. I promise you. I cannot say when right yet but we will go," Rosa said.

"This is correct," Armando said. "It won't be long. Not this summer maybe but sometime soon. I promise."

"Oooh, I hope so," Maria said drearily.

Late in the evening, Armando sat alone in the living room. Rosa came by and said she would be happy to sit with him if he would like but Armando said he would rather be alone and think about everything that had happened recently.

"If you wish, love. But don't stay up too late," she said.

Soft yellow light from the streetlamp came

in the window filling the room with a friendly glow. Armando felt both happy and sad. Happy that he had finally taken the initiative to move forward on his dream rather than to talk about it day after day, week after week, year after year. But sad as well. Sad that it did not go well at the bank. He had set his expectations very high, yet he knew Rosa and Billie Doyle were right when they told him not to be discouraged by the decision of the bank. He knew that if he had to go to a hundred banks Rosa would support him through it all. *She is a very strong person*, he said to himself. *I am lucky to have her as my wife. She is the heart and the soul of the family. I cannot imagine what it would be like without her. I don't want to even consider it.*

The ambiance of the room was like a tranquil vapor that spread around him. A cleansing vapor that scrubbed away his doubts and brought him courage. He closed his eyes. When he was on the rooftops he never lacked courage even though many of the jobs were difficult and dangerous.

But the courage Rosa had was different. He saw how it came into every part of her life. She had the kind of courage that only mothers and wives have. Armando knew this. He had seen it from their first days together in Corpus Christi. He knew it was the same courage that his mother had in Saltillo while raising a family without a husband. Armando worshipped the courage he saw in Rosa and his mother. *Perhaps it is a rare trait that is given to women by God*, he thought. *As long as Rosa believes I can succeed, then I know I will*, he told himself. He recalled the resiliency Rosa had when he told her about the bad news Burkhart had given him at the bank—how she would not let the setback discourage him.

Armando thought back to the day in Saltillo when he decided to come to America. The day he broke the news to his mother and how she supported his decision because she knew it was good for him. There was no future and little hope for a better life for Armando in the tile factories.

And he thought about the day he crossed the border into America, almost alone. He remembered it as though it were yesterday. Now he could laugh about it because he was the only true wetback in the family. Not Carlos or Maria or Rosa. He was the wetback. He laughed.

When he came to America he knew he would have to work with his hands and his back and this did not bother him because he was used to it. Maybe he would even have to dig ditches— it did not matter to him. Someday his dream would come true in America.

Yes, he had spent his life working with his hands and his back. But he was happy to do it because he knew that Carlos would never have to dig ditches or climb onto scorching hot roofs. He knew that Maria would not have to clean the houses of the rich and take care of their children. Their dreams were big, but most of all, their dreams could be achieved. Maria could become a surgeon someday if she worked hard and didn't give up on her dream. And Carlos could even become a Senator someday if he wanted to. Armando had faith in his children. He was proud of how hard they worked in school and how they were rewarded by getting good grades in all their classes—the easy ones and the difficult ones alike.

Armando looked at his watch. "Oh my, almost one o'clock and another hard day tomorrow," he uttered. He went quietly up to the bedroom and climbed into bed and gave Rosa a soft kiss. "I love you, my dear," he said, and fell quickly into a deep and restful sleep on the cool sheets.

11

Nothing changed during the rest of August except that each day seemed hotter than the one before and each day Armando felt older than the day before. As he drove west on Bellaire Boulevard he thought about that. *I am now barely forty years old but being on the rooftops for so many years has made me grow old very quickly.*

Even so, he thought good thoughts as he sped down the street, cars tight up behind him and in front of him. *I am lucky to work for Billie and Charlie Doyle almost full time now.* The thought of that lifted his spirits and even brought a smile to his face. He looked at the palm of his hand and saw callouses and bruises. But that too made him laugh. A good thought passed across his mind: *Any time now. I don't know when but soon Perfect Roofing will have many roofing jobs right here in Houston. And just like Billie Doyle told me, we will get many more jobs from the people whose houses we have worked on, from the recommendations of others.* Thinking of that, he could ignore the burst of crazy traffic that weaved back and forth around him.

For three weeks Armando visited one bank after another. Each time the news that came back was not good. Some banks said he needed a marketing plan even though he had put one together with the help of a friend who knew how to do it. One bank said he needed a lawyer. "What if you were to get sued or if someone got hurt?" the banker said. "You need to be ready for every possibility if you are going to work for yourself. All companies need lawyers."

Rosa worked with a woman whose husband was a lawyer. He told Armando he could use his name when talking to the bankers. But even that did not satisfy some of the banks. Armando felt as though he was going in circles from bank to bank with no success. One by one his chance at the American dream seemed to be fading away.

After many weeks and many visits to many banks he told Rosa, "I don't think I will ever succeed. I don't think so." He sat at the kitchen table leaning forward, shoulders down, massaging the callouses on his palms.

"Oh, Armando, don't say that," Rosa said, sitting at the table with him. "Think how long you have wanted to do this. Think about it. From the very moment you came to America…even before. Are you going to give up now? Well?"

After a while, Armando said, "Maybe I am not so sure the American dream is real. Maybe I just imagined it. It is true for very rich people. I think that is the case. But they are already living the American dream. So perhaps it is time to forget about it." Armando shrugged and shook his head. "Perhaps."

"If you give up now, then what? Will you put shingles on the roof for other people the rest of your life?"

Armando continued to rub his hands. "I don't know. Somehow I feel like the banks are being unfair to us," he uttered.

Rosa, too, felt this now and then but she did not tell Armando. She always taught Carlos and Maria that just because things are not going your way it does not mean that you are being discriminated against.

"We will keep trying. We will keep trying until you succeed," Rosa said.

Armando knew Rosa would say that and it made him smile a little. "What if we sold the house and used the money for the company?" he said. "We could move into an apartment for a while and then when all is going well, when the company is making money, we can buy another house. Maybe even a bigger and fancier house."

"Oh, no, no. We can never do that, Armando," Rosa insisted. "We worked our whole life to own this house and *now* it is ours. We don't want to start over again. Everything will work out. I know it will. I am very confident. Very, very confident. I am."

"You're right. I would never want to give up this house. And besides, it is very important that Carlos and Maria have a good place to live."

Rosa said, "I always say that I am sorry I never met your mother. I truly wish I had. But tell me, what would she say at a time like this?"

Armando did not think for long before replying, "She would say: 'Don't get discouraged, Armando. Always believe in your dreams.'"

"And yes, love, that is what we will do. We will continue to believe in your dream and not give up."

This made Armando feel better. He was sure he could continue forward even if there were many more setbacks.

Still, disappointments continued to pile up. Each visit to a new bank went as badly as the others, sometimes worse.

One day after work when the crew had left Billie Doyle again asked Armando how things were going. They sat on the grass, warm from the day's heat, under a large elm tree.

"Terrible," Armando said somberly. "I don't know what's wrong. I've hit a brick wall, it seems."

"I may know what's going on," Billie Doyle said. "Something similar happened to me and Chahlie when we were in Boston. You see, we're from the south of Boston, a place they call Southie. Mostly kids from Irish families. For many, many years even until today people from Southie have been treated badly. The Irish in Southie are not liked by a lot of the people in Boston. You wouldn't think this would happen today, would you? But it does. Well…Chahlie and me had a hell of a lot of trouble getting a loan, just like you're having now. Eventually an uncle of ours coughed up enough money for us to get a start. But that turned out to be only half the problem. The next problem was we couldn't get jobs. It should've been easy but it wasn't. Boston is a city of many neighborhoods and many suburbs with old houses. And just like here in Houston roofs go bad and need to be replaced. But few people wanted to hire us. Soon as we opened our mouths people could tell we were from Southie. Believe me, it's very evident if you live in Boston. So that was another battle we had to fight for a while."

Armando was amazed. He thought people as decent as Billie and Charlie Doyle would never have trouble getting work no matter where they were.

"But we stuck it out and finally succeeded. Then after a couple of years, Chahlie said we should get away from Boston. I know it's hot as shit on the roofs here in Houston in the summer but you should see what it's like on a rooftop in Cambridge or Somerville or Watertown or Dorchester in December or January or February. Layers of ice and snow. We heard that there was roofing work here in Houston so we packed up and came out. That was eight years ago now."

Armando appreciated the tale but had no idea why Billie Doyle bothered to tell it to him.

"Maybe you've been hitting the wrong banks," Billie Doyle said. "That's my hunch."

"I've been going to all the banks in the area and some in other parts of the city."

"Okay, amigo, let's try this." Billie Doyle pulled out his wallet and retrieved a business card and handed it to Armando. "Here is the bank we work with. They know us very well. Make an appointment to see this fella." He tapped the card. "He's a very good guy. You might have better luck."

Armando stared at the card, holding it as if it had special magic of some sort.

"Well, it's late and still very hot. Tomorrow is another day of work." Billie Doyle shook Armando's hand and walked to his truck.

That night, Armando told Rosa about his conversation with Billie. He showed her the card he had given Armando and said he would make an appointment as soon as possible.

"Billie did not have to do this," Armando said. "He is a very nice and very generous man. He might even refer some work to us. That's what I feel. They always have a lot of business, almost more than they can handle. But first I will go to the bank he recommended. That's the reason he gave me the card and there was no mistake of it. Yes, Billie Doyle is a very good man. Both of them are, Billie and Charlie. They are the kind of people that make up for bastards like Herrera."

Armando worked the rest of the week for Billie and Charlie Doyle. On his lunch hour he called the man at the bank on the card that Billie Doyle had given him and made an appointment for Saturday.

When Armando walked into the bank, he felt more comfortable speaking with bankers, and that helped. His presentation came off smoothly and professionally. He had a good marketing plan, an insurance company that would provide coverage in the event something happened to a worker or the house, the name of a lawyer from a friend Rosa worked with. Armando knew he had a strong case and he felt very confident—even more so because of the recommendation from Billie Doyle. Armando spent over an hour with the banker. The banker made no mistake about his desire to help people like Armando.

"We take pride in making it possible for people to get a start in business, Mr. Ortiz," the banker said. "We, here at the bank, believe that small businesses are the life blood of the economy. I will look your application over very carefully but from what I can tell so far you have planned it out quite well." He looked at Armando, and said, "Mr. Ortiz, I don't know if you are aware, but Billie and Charlie Doyle were in here a few days ago going over some matters for their company. We've worked with them for years. While they were here they put in a good word for you…said they hoped we might be able to help you get a start."

All of Armando's life he had a sixth sense for seeing into the soul of a person. He saw simple and truthful sincerity in the face of the man who sat across from him. Armando was convinced his dream would finally come true, that this would be the day his life would change forever.

"So give us a few days if you can and we'll get back to you," the man said. He stood up and shook Armando's hand genially.

Three days later the banker called and asked Armando to stop in for a visit. Armando donned his suit and tie and went the bank as he had done to dozens of other banks previously. This time, the news was good. The bank would grant Armando a loan. Armando could barely contain the joy he felt.

Returning home, there were few wild and frantic cars speeding along as would happen in the mornings and evenings during the week. The air outside was steamy and hot like every other day in August but today at least Armando was glad not to be on a rooftop.

His thoughts ran back to the day he met Rosa in Corpus Christi. He still remembered what he said to her at the dance at St. Michael's Church, that it was his desire, his hope, his dream even as a boy growing up in Mexico to someday start a business of his own. He did not know exactly what kind of business. Something in construction probably because it was what he knew best. He was always good at working with his hands.

His journey to achieve his goal had been long and difficult. At times he even wondered if perhaps it would have been better if he had stayed in Saltillo. He could have remained at the tile factory, possibly even becoming a foreman someday. He could have made a decent living doing that. A simple but decent living. True, there was not much future in it, as his mother had told him many times. But life in Mexico was simple and less complicated. *Dreams are wonderful to have*, Armando occasionally thought. But he also knew that dreams can trick us. Can make us believe that life will be better than what it is now. Armando knew that dreams can fool us.

Yet, Armando was sure that leaving Mexico had been the right decision. Had he not come to America he never would have met Rosa, the most spectacular person on the planet in the eyes of Armando. And he would not have Carlos and Maria, who gave him great joy every day of his life. Yes, he had truly made the right decision. And yes, even though he had to spend many years on the red-hot rooftops, it had been worth it.

Armando was sure that today was the day Perfect Roofing would become more than the dream he had hoped for his whole life. The American dream. He knew that Perfect Roofing would be a good and decent company like the one Billie and Charlie Doyle owned. Thinking of that brought a tear to his eye. He brushed it away and laughed as he drove along the boulevard glancing up now and then at the sun that broiling above him.